Sister

Sister

A Novel by Jim Lewis

Karma

Copyright © 2016 Jim Lewis

Published by Karma, New York

Originally published by Graywolf Press in 1993

ISBN 978-1-942607-44-1

Cover image © Christopher Wool

The author would like to thank Brendan Dugan and the people at Karma for their
kindness and cooperation, and Christopher Wool for creating the cover image.

Library of Congress Cataloging-in-Publication Data:

Lewis, Jim
Sister: a novel / by Jim Lewis
p. cm.
ISBN 1-55597-178-4
I. Title.
PS3562.E9475S54 1993
813'.54—dc20 92-34194

To my father and mother.
For my friends.

Preface

A life of rational planning, a happy life that owes nothing to luck, is necessarily independent of others; so it's a life without love, without deep company. There are careers devoted to indiscernible causes, to mere thinking or interminable prayer. They are not ours. There are hermits who prefer their seaside caves, armies made of forgotten mercenaries, astronomers who see only stars. But for us one motion of individual want sends trembles around a circle of dependents, until the whole helpless ring knocks and shakes like a tray of wine glasses in an unsteady waiter's hands. Any music they might make is random, involuntary and brief: one can't be still unless they all are, and they never are. How unbearable.

It's true I'm a singular creature, a mooncalf, a monster if you will, equally knocked about and knocking. I have been and I've known as much for as long as I can remember, and I remember everything. Still, I don't know why: maybe my mother had a scare while she was carrying me, or some cold spirit or spirochete wended its way into my company during the first days of my term, or some gene jumped from its proper place. Something happened, something moved or went astray and marked me as I lay there bathing blindly. I don't know: I have no myth or miracle to sustain me or help me understand, so I sustain myself with these idle dreams and inventions, and wonder if the weather will end. It hasn't ended yet.

My name is Wilson. Once when I was young I knew a pair of fierce young girls, was taken by one for love and by the other for rage, and we rattled the glasses until they broke. That's my story. I will pursue it now like a boy chasing an errant firefly with open hands on a dark summer lawn.

One Mississippi

1

On my seventeenth birthday I left my home in Lincoln, Nebraska, and went out for a walk into the world. It was a clear day, a Friday late in March. The sky was a deep and noble blue, the sun was invisibly bright, and the air was warming, though the shifting breeze still harbored traces of winter's bitterness. As birds chirruped outside my window I threw some clothes, a toothbrush, and a book into a large duffel bag, and then I closed up my house, locked it carefully, crossed the brown lawn beneath the still-bare trees, and without a last look back started down the muddy road. I was heading south towards the summer and whatever waited for me there; it had been years since I'd been able to tell a day when I wondered about it from a day.

There was a spring in my step as I passed the end of the city, and for a few hours I walked along the shoulder of Highway 80, heading east past the city limits, past the intersection where it met the road north, past the final mile of strip malls, gas stations, motels and convenience stores. Soon there was nothing to watch but the fence posts and farmhouses, so I began to sing a song of my own invention:

> Snakes are quick and crows are bold
> Rain is wet and snow is cold
> Coal is black and gold is gold
> I'll be young until I'm old.

Over and over again I sang my little verselet, with the mood changing according to the slow entrances of opportuning noise; as I went by a herd of mooing cows it became a chorale, then it rocked with the rattle of chains on a passing truck, and as an airplane passed slowly overhead the drone added a meditative touch. This last tone lingered for a few minutes after the plane had disappeared, leaving me content and happily humming, and when a fat man in a beat-up station wagon took it upon himself to pull his car to the side of the road and ask me if I needed a lift, I thanked him and said No.

He tipped his cap back on his forehead and without a word started off again, leaving me to myself.

As I went on my mind wandered, from the home I'd left behind to the world I hoped I would find ahead, and most of the day had disappeared beneath my feet before my thoughts were interrupted: I looked up from the ground as I rounded a long bend and saw a line of trucks parked out in a field by the side of the road, with their cargo spilled out onto the grass: it was a carnival under construction. In the fading light of day the multicolored fights and bright paint seemed like futile stuff, no match for the amber afternoon. A Ferris wheel already rode above the grass, with its dark spokes spinning in place; next to it was a spider-armed contraption holding motionless cars; then a jerry-built street lined with painted booths, and a series of commission carts standing by the side, waiting for night and the folks who would make their way out in the darkness, their pockets filled with jangling coins. As I passed I could hear faint candy-colored music coming from the far end, but I kept walking; I was afraid some barker might spot me slouching across the state and come out to the highway to sign me up.

I wouldn't have stopped, no matter what he offered: I was looking for some concoction of pleasure and peace, a bottle full of unstable combinations, sealed like a pharmacist's healing syrup to prevent the fragile base from evaporating. My song went:

What's yours is yours, what's mine is mine
And I don't mind dying
—No, I don't mind.

2

In time the houses thinned out, and as evening began to fall I came upon an abandoned farmhouse. I couldn't tell how long it had been since a farmer had lived there and cared for the place, but it must have been a while: the house had been reduced to tatters by the weather, shutters hung slantwise from the face by single screws, and all that was left of the roof were strips of fading tar paper. On the ground by the side door there was a small pile of bricks that had once been a chimney. In places I caught glimpses of the horizon through missing slats in the walls, as if the house was a half-solved puzzle—Complete the Picture, or Find the Hidden Face—in a Sunday supplement. It seemed an inviting place to spend the night, so I walked up to the front fence and hied myself over it and into the mud in the yard.

I'd just started towards the doorway when—lo!—a group of pigs came trotting around from behind a backyard shed, big, black creatures with plug eyes and brutish snouts. They drove one another back and forth across the ground as they came towards me on their piggy-sharp feet. Ha! I yelled, and they broke into a seesaw gallop and abruptly turned away, kicking up clods of mud as they collided, and giving out with grunts and alarmed squeals. Their voices became dimmer as they disappeared around a corner, and then at last it was quiet again. There was no door to the house at all, and I found more pigs inside, lying lazily in the rooms; one turned her face up to look at me, snuffled loudly, and then dropped her head again and went back to sleep. I could hear the heavy scuffling of hooves on distant floorboards and feel the lingering heat from their hides; I could smell the deep odor of mud, of shit and sweet hay. There was a cast-iron stove lying on its side in the living room, and the door to the kitchen had been pulled off its hinges and propped against a wall. I made my way to the hallway and started upstairs, stepping carefully over the missing boards. On the second floor I found a landing, two or three decrepit rooms, and a second flight of stairs disappearing up into a dark attic, above which, through two separate holes in the roof, I could see the sky, already faded and softened like well-washed cloth. I put my pack down in one corner of the master bedroom and sat beside it with my back propped against a wall.

It was growing dark out; there was a mighty grey on the plains, and the air was suddenly flushed. From the open window I could see clouds gathering in the sky, grey-green with rain and electricity:

it was as if my room were the housing inside some giant, archaic experimental apparatus, and I was the quivering element. I lay myself down in a corner, pulled my shoes off, put my pack under my neck with the sharp corner of my book pressed into my shoulder, and listened to the cars passing from time to time on the road outside. Shush . . . the sky thickened, a few fat drops fell at the head of night's advancing column, and then a full parade of rain began, to celebrate my first day of independence.

3

That night I dreamed about a man with arms that were wings. When I saw him his hair was burned and his skin blackened from some punishing fire that escaped his belief, as if he would always wonder what he'd done wrong. I was lying on my back and he came down to me suddenly, wrapped in a cloud of luminous mist amid which sheets of fire snapped in the wind, as if he were a refugee running from some imaginary, superlunar war. I was afraid he was going to speak, afraid of whatever blessing or brief he might bring, but he was empty-handed and silent. He looked at me, pecked once at my hip, and then bent his head down until it rested on his birdlike breast. Then he hid his face under the feathers, not out of shame, but as if to prevent me from recognizing him. I was so transfixed by the sight that I couldn't move; nor did he stir again; and the dream went on in a kind of stasis, as if some mechanism were stuck, until finally it began to fade, the figure slowly dissolving into a smear of grey and black. At the end the light flickered, until at last it was dark. I slept on another hour or two without any companion but the cold.

When I woke up it was morning and the room was bright with sunshine, and smelled of charred hair. There were ashes scattered across the floor; my back was stiff. In the opposite corner my visitor slept, with his arms folded over his chest and his body curled in on itself under a blue army jacket. I lay there, drowsy and half-awake for a few minutes, and watched him as he dreamed, thinking maybe

16

it was me. I had my leg cramped beneath me, and I slowly stretched it out, too tired to rise. He turned over and briefly shook himself. Shuffle, edit. In time he opened his eyes and turned his small head towards me until I could see his face; it was expressionless, sallow and worn, and the flesh of his features hung from its bones so that his thin mouth dangled open. I could hear his short, fast breaths escaping. He was a grotesque, with his tiny, yellow eyes, dull hair, and his body bent and damaged.

As soon as he seemed to be awake enough to hear me I greeted him, but he didn't answer, didn't even nod or shake his head; still, his eyes moved from my face to the corners of the room, and then back again, and he put one small finger up to the side of his beak, bent over, and abruptly blew out the contents on the floor beside his bed. Then he got up and began to dress. I watched him as he hid his long, thin limbs underneath a flannel shirt with a tear in the sleeve and then pulled on a filthy wool overcoat, which he buttoned all the way up with cold, fumbling fingers. He had no hat.

I got up and splashed some water on my face from a puddle under a leak in the roof, and then began gathering my things into the bag. By the time I'd finished he was standing shyly in his corner of the room beside a hole in the floorboards, beneath which I could see the fat black hillocks of the pigs as they rooted into the corners of the living room below. I motioned to him and he raised his eyebrows, but he didn't move, so I approached him and reached my hand out slowly. He offered his forearm to me like a blind man, and I felt the fragile bones beneath his clothing as my fingers closed around it; and then in soft slow motion I drew him out of the room and into the hallway, and we made our way to the head of the stairs. Together we paused while I shook the last sleep from my eyes, and then, while he leaned lightly on my arm, I guided him slowly down the steps with me, each one in turn, as if, like a cat caught in a tree, he'd scrambled up and couldn't get to the ground again without my help.

We stood together on the ground before the house, blinking in the clear blue light, with the morning horizon ahead of us and the night horizon behind, while the sky opened mechanically overhead like the slow ocular roof of an observatory. It was too early in the morning for there to be any traffic, so we crossed the yard, climbed carefully over the fence, and began down the road on foot, my paces outmeasuring his by half. After a mile or so had passed I stopped to look back at the house for one last time, perched there on the barren crest of the globe like the poorhouse in a cautionary fable. When I turned back again I found my companion staring at me with black pupils set in a yellowish cast. He quickly averted his eyes when my gaze met his. I'm not one to be looked at, he said.

I'm not either, I replied, and we set off again. As we walked I explained myself. I told him that I was a doctor's son, and that I'd left what home I'd had a year or two after my father died. I told him about my pursuit. I said I was prepared to ride as far south as Mexico. The country, I said, was open below me like a stadium from the stands.

He nodded each time I paused, but when I told him I'd dreamed about him the night before he immediately stopped, turned to me wide-eyed, and said No! so forcefully that I shut my mouth. We passed a few long minutes in a silence broken only by the cold, quiet grinding of the gravel beneath our feet. A car.

Today is Saturday? he asked.

March twenty-first.

That makes it a fucking month, he said, and kicked a dun-colored stone out onto the blacktop. That seemed to be all he could come up with for the moment, so I waited. A yellow tractor went past, leaving behind parallel chevron-shaped mud tracks on the road, a small plume of black exhaust in the blue air, and a slowly Dopplering rumble in between. I could feel him gathering himself, drawing in the particles of his confidence and molding them into an invisible substance within him, and when the mass was reached he stopped again and cleared his throat with a rattle. Have you got any money? he said while he stared at the rubber marks where a car had skidded off the road. I reached into my pocket for a coin, but I thought better of it when I caught the look on his face, and instead I fetched my wallet out of my jacket, plucked out a bill, and turned it over to him. He treated the note as if it might be made of flash paper, holding it between his fingertips and watching it for a moment to see if it would disappear in a burst of pale green, spendthrift light. When he was satisfied that it was immutable he folded it carefully and tucked it into the breast pocket of his shirt.

He began to walk again, but I stopped him by putting my hand on his chest and I asked him his name. Well . . . he paused and cocked his head. Jones, he said, then he shrugged.

Jones, I said. All right. He looked out across the field at the horizon. Are you leaving?

I guess I am, he said, as he reached out and took my hand in his. It was dead cold and dry. Then he leaned forward, tugged my arm until I stood above him and my face passed a shadow over his, reached up on his toes, and kissed my mouth . . . I could feel the sun on my neck and his heart beating against my chest, smell his dirty breath, see his white eyelids lowered an inch from mine. It was a long moment before he released me from his grasp, and when he did he turned and started out into the field by the side of the road. I stood on the shoulder and watched him for a while as he walked out into the long grass, tilting from side to side on his paces, until he dwindled into a dark point and then disappeared. I could taste the salt and smell of his mouth all morning.

4

I walked alone for a few hours, a raggedy man by the side of the road, covered in dust from the rigs that blew past me. By mid-afternoon I'd come to a small town over the crest of a dry hill. In the general store I bought a sandwich and a bus ticket to Chicago. I was a sightly thing, but the woman behind the counter was passing time with a delivery man, and she would have sold passage to the devil himself without noticing.

I'm going down to Reno in June, said the man, gesturing towards my ticket as she filled it out. She had one of those Midwestern faces that looks like it's been drawn on a balloon; the string jerked and she nodded. He leaned over the counter and began to watch what she was doing, as if he was thinking of applying for a job along the same lines and wanted to see what it would take. Get a cheap ticket down and try my luck.

Oh, boy, she said. Just don't sit there and lose everything. My friend Katey . . . She turned the ticket around and slid it across to me, then disappeared behind the refrigerator case. He pulled a pack of cigarettes out of his shirt pocket and lit one, shiffed his breath in through his teeth, and sighed out a small plume of ashen smoke.

Fifteen-fifty, she said to me when she returned. They stood quietly while I counted out the money, but neither of them looked at me; they were simply being polite to my parting wages. He scanned the covers of the magazines in the rack beside him, and as I took the bag and started for the door he pointed to a copy of a tabloid and made a comment that I missed, and she laughed so loudly that I looked back, and saw her hand clasped over her mouth to keep her teeth from showing.

As I sat on the curb outside and waited a state trooper's car pulled to the corner and stopped. The signal changed to green, but the car didn't move; the officer had his head tipped up while he watched me through his rearview mirror. I brought out my sandwich and slowly unwrapped it. The signal was red again. A blackbird on a telephone wire across the way raised his wings and started up into the sky, and I removed a flaccid green spear of pickle from the waxed paper and deposited it back in the bag. When the signal changed the trooper pulled away from the curb, made a U-turn, and disappeared. The bus was the next vehicle to heave up the road.

It was night when I arrived in Chicago, and the city was glittering in the misty sky, hovering like an enormous craft in the hot, tangerine glow of its own illumination. I immediately felt a kind of rapture, and I spent an hour or two just wandering north, ducking past the pedestrians on the narrow sidewalks, stopping to stare through a store window. When the lights and the traffic began to thin out, I turned right and strolled over a few blocks, crossing the highway and making my way across a wide strip of grass until I reached the deep edge of the lake. There were orange lights out in the water, the faint sound of wavelets sipping at the shore. As I walked south along the stone wall I came upon a man and a woman, lying out in the darkness. She was long-limbed and red-haired, and she was stretched out on her back with her hands clasped behind her head. He was half-reclined beside her. As I approached I heard him laugh as she said, I hit him with a piece of, like the thing from a bicycle. I must have been eleven. The black lake swelled up to meet the black sky. Slowly he bent over her, big-shouldered and dark. She closed her eyes, smiled slightly, and let him gently kiss her. Then she pushed him away and sat up, looked quickly at me, and pulled her white jacket around her middle. Molly, he said, and started to protest, but she shushed him softly as I passed.

The depot was empty by the time I made my way back. According to the clock over the door it was two in the morning; according to another near the ticket windows it was ten to three. For a few hours I slept on a brown bench in the waiting room, dreaming quick, static dreams interrupted by night's obscure motions around my real body, until they melted together into a single strange document in which the pictures don't illustrate the words. When I woke up the next morning there were people all around, making a traffic island out of my bed. I caught the first bus south.

It was seven hours just to Missouri, and I dozed by the window as the blue fields and small towns passed. For a while we raced a train on a set of tracks beside the highway; we gradually lost. My first seat-mate, a silent man with a long, pale face, disappeared somewhere in the lower Illinois plains, leaving behind a Chicago newspaper that car sickness prevented me from reading. My second was a sweaty woman with a fidgety daughter across the aisle, whom she ignored until the shining parabola of the St. Louis arch appeared on the horizon. Is that where Grandma lives? asked the girl. It's not Grandma, it's Julie, her mother snapped. Now hush up.

And I remember Memphis the following day, the bus stop a tin building on the south end of town where we sat for an hour or so. The driver left the engine idling, and it rumbled as if it were restless. Across the road there was a diner, and I stretched my legs and stopped in for some listless breakfast, taking a booth so I could stare out the window. We were at an intersection and it was the middle of a weekday morning; a pickup passed with an old man planted in the driver's seat, staring carefully out through the windshield, his hands gripping the wheel. There were some black children walking in the street, laughing, and a teenage boy lying back on the hood of his car in the parking lot of the gas station across the street.

South of Memphis the highway rose and sank as it passed through uneven fields. From time to time the bus would pull over to an exit, and we'd take a few minutes to stop at some small town and drop off a passenger. We were headed towards Louisiana when I first saw the Mississippi River in daylight, running wide, great and brown at the edge of the highway, a thick spine, storied home to Br'er Rabbit, and John Henry, and Stagger Lee. We followed by its bank for a few hours, and then the driver turned off to stop in a small city that spread east from the bluffs.

It was the countyseat, a few hundred years settled, and there was profit there, collected like silt from the river; I could see it in the big old houses we passed, in the neat shops and flush air of the townspeople as they went about their business. When we pulled into the depot I asked the driver to get my bag from beneath the bus. Your ticket's to Houston, he said as he climbed down from his seat. You sure? I was sure: I had felt a prescient shiver, a bit of uncaused knowledge as I sat, and I believed it was the right place for me to settle.

Diesel smoke hung in the afternoon air, and a few cabdrivers leaned against their cars. One of them answered my first question by pointing across the highway to a motel. I scrambled between the traffic, and within a minute I was in a room with my bags dropped inside the door. After I showered and shaved I turned the television on and began a nap that lasted until I was awakened by the sound of the couple next door arguing. From the window I looked out into the alley and the houses beyond, anonymous buildings with shut windows and broken roofs, left in a pile beneath the darkening sky like playthings on the floor of some busy child's bedroom. With one fingertip I tapped the glass a few times, and then I turned away and went to bed.

5

The city was small enough that I could circle it in a long day's walk; I would leave my room in the morning, stroll from one end of the shopping district to the next, and then hike out for a mile or so to the high school and come back around, past pretty churches and quiet, carefully trimmed lawns, and I was always home before dinner. Each day I made a slightly different course, down shady streets fragrant with magnolias and oaks, across a footbridge that spanned the highway, along a path above the river. Within a week I had the whole town fixed in my mind, and I bought a copy of the local paper.

That first morning I went looking for a place to stay, and by noon I'd taken a room above the garage behind a house on the south side of town. My landlady was an elderly woman who lived alone among the sort of impeccable furnishings that only those one step above ruin bother to maintain; every picture and brass lamp was perfectly placed, the carpets were newly vacuumed, the curtains were drawn just so, as if housekeeping alone would keep the specter of poverty away. I don't usually take in tenants, she had said as she sat me down with a cup of tea at one end of a firm couch and slowly lowered herself onto the other end. I just have to these days—she quickly glanced at the floor—because my paycheck, I work for the local school board, you know, isn't enough, even with my husband's pension. I set the cup of tea down on a coaster and nodded. Anyway, she continued, you seem like a nice young man. She paused for a second as if waiting for me to contradict her, and I suddenly noticed, from the tentative way she reached for the plate of cookies on the table before us, that without the glasses suspended from a string around her neck she was nearly blind. Would you like one? she asked. I said, No, thank you, and she set them down again carefully.

As she walked me up an outside set of stairs to a room above the garage she talked on about the town and its history and what there was for a fellow like me to do there. I don't get out much myself, she said as she fumbled with a rusty key in the rusty lock. They were lines from a country movie that she had memorized years before, and she played the part slightly nervously, as if she were trying to please a director in the shadows over my shoulder. Things were certainly different when my husband was alive. You couldn't keep me in then.

The room was small and the ceiling was low, and as I listened to her I looked around; there was a bed and a desk, and through a half-open door at the top of a few stairs I glimpsed the corner of a small, dark bathroom. She reached up to touch a polished lens, and asked me if everything was to my liking. I said it was and dropped my bag down on the bed, and she resumed her talk.

Age bores some into quietude; others it makes chatter like bone white dice on a hardtop table. She went on for a while . . .. Somewhere outside a phone began to ring, rang and rang, and stopped. The sun moved a shadow from the window frame across a stain on the floorboards. Thank you, ma'am: long company is a lesson in time's disorder, which every lingering child must learn someday. Well, I won't bore you anymore, she said at last, but if you need anything you just come down and ask me.

6

The next morning I walked into town, bought a paper from a newsstand, and settled down to breakfast in a hotel restaurant. Weather mild, the bond bill failed, a suspicious fire in a riverside warehouse, Congress debates the law of averages. When I reached the help wanted ads I began to circle the paragraphs. At midmorning I called a gardening firm called Turner's from a phone booth on the street; just after lunch I stopped by (berry blue trucks in the parking lot, grass green bench inside) and had a short interview with a distracted manager. Ageless, boyish, mannish, mischievous, I added a full seven years to my age. He never bothered to look up from my application, and I was hired to start as an assistant the next day.

At first it was just work, and no more. With the dispatcher's assignment in hand by ten we used to arrive at a house by midmorning, park in the driveway, and get straight to it. I was on my knees pulling weeds in the morning, planting bulbs in the afternoon, mowing lawns in the evening. I was left alone most of the time, and before long I'd found a rhythm that helped me pass the days effortlessly. It's true I hadn't settled into a proper life—I had no friends, no pastime—but I didn't worry. On the bus to work one morning I spotted an old Ford in a passing driveway, with a hand-lettered FOR SALE sign in the window. I went back for a second look that evening; it seemed solid enough, so I rang the doorbell and asked after it. The owner was an eccentric, excitable man with a white, waxed mustache who jabbered as he popped the hood and touched each of the engine's parts as if they were talismans. As I counted out the money into his open hand he danced from one foot to the other, and as I drove off I saw him in the mirror, waving good-bye.

7

Standing on the deck of a standing ship, a sailor looks for coming waves in the subtle swells of the grey-green horizon. The dark water rises far in the distance, and he waits for the long causes to build—but it's simply the random motion of the sea; it never approaches; it has no effect. So I stood and watched for my future, looking for a reason in the distance that would pick me up like a wave and bring me up onto the shore. It never came: instead, a creeping tide, an undertow, moved me quietly along.

One morning about a month after I'd started work I received a new assignment. Wilson! the dispatcher said sharply, and as I approached he wiped his hands on his shirt before picking up the yellow slip that lay on the desk in front of him. Scratch. He folded it carefully in two, flattened the crease with a dirty thumbnail, and pushed it through the mouse hole in the bottom of his window. Brand new, he said. Don't fuck it up.

The address was far down a street called Cypress. I remembered it from my first survey of the town; it was on a hill that began where the playing fields of the public high school ended, and as our truck rattled through the wide, tidy rambles, with their wrought-iron lamp-posts and broad sidewalks, their centuries-old trees making dappled shadows on the unbroken asphalt, I rolled down my window and took in the confident scent of lawns and flowers, and I remember wondering what hidden manufacture made such perfume possible.

The house itself was hidden behind tall, well-groomed hedges, marked only by a yellow barn-shaped mailbox with a nameplate that said The Millers. I stopped, shifted into half gear, lurched, shifted again, and started to nose the truck into the driveway just in time to miss colliding with a mouse-grey sedan that was coming down. The driver, a plump man with a grey beard, braked and pulled to one side, then waved to us peremptorily as we passed.

The oaks that lined the driveway were hung with Spanish moss, but the house itself was nowhere to be seen, only knotted branches with their mannered freight, and between the rough trunks the edge of an immaculate lawn. A quarter of a mile passed before the trees parted to reveal a great wooden frame in the shape of an octagon, with windows on every side, columns before the door, and a balcony with a white railing on the second floor. I brought the truck to a stop, quietly, gently, so as not to break the glassy picture into pieces, and my partners and I got down from the cab to survey the place.

The grounds were cast back behind the house with the ease and grandeur of a kept woman's blanket thrown lazily over her bed. Out the kitchen door there was a patio built of flagstones, which ended in a strip of grass leading to a stone square with a small fountain in the middle. To one side of the square there was an herb garden, flanked with myrtle trees. To the other there was a hedgerow, and beyond it a long, gentle slope leading down to a few rows of flower beds, azaleas arranged so that paths of turf waded through them, and daffodils, camellias, begonias, and tea roses. On the far side, away from the house, the square ended in a short flight of brick steps, after which there was a wide, rolling field dotted with flowering dogwood, and among the boxwoods at the end there was a small pond stocked with goldfish, with a wrought-iron bench beside it. At the very bottom of the garden, as far away from the house as possible, a large gazebo, long in disrepair, peeked out from behind a large willow tree.

We spent the rest of the day poking around and preparing: the lawn had grown long since the last workers had been by, and the edges of the flower beds were ragged. From time to time I'd see a shade that slipped into the house behind the slamming of a screen door, or the flash of an anonymous midriff exposed as a window was raised, but aside from those glimpses there might have been no one there at all. The grounds were so large that a shout at one end wouldn't be heard at the other, and the house presented such a diffuse facade, as if to scatter attention back into the garden around it, that it seemed more a monument, solid, sufficient, and uninhabited, than a dwelling. But it was the garden, rather than the house in it, that enthralled me. It was as big as a mother's pride, and it was still untested. It begged for me, and I knew right away that it was the medium of my next years: I loved the place, and I vowed that afternoon to do whatever I could to keep it in my purview.

Over the following two weeks I made such a show of my efforts that I managed to have myself assigned there regularly, and soon it was simply understood that the Millers' garden was Wilson's trust, and Wilson's song was:

It's hard to know, it's hard to say
How we ended up this way
But work we must if work we can
Down to the last poor powerless man.

In the evening I would return to my room, wash my hands, fix myself dinner, and sleep.

8

My landlady had a back neighbor, a plump, white-haired old woman who was as deaf as my landlady was blind, though she didn't have the gadget to correct it. One weekend afternoon I'd helped her by moving a compost heap from one side of her tiny, perfect garden to the other, and I'd listened to her singsong mumbles the whole time without once understanding a full phrase. From that afternoon on I was her second-best friend, and she used to hang her head over the fence behind the garage and watch me with her watery eyes as I walked up the stairs to my apartment. When I was halfway up she would call to me—well, not my name, but some collection of consonants—and I'd turn and watch her gesture as if she were trying to initiate me into some urgent, secret, and solitary society. I never knew why she was beckoning, but I'd come down the stairs again until I was close enough for her to reach through the fence for my shirttail, which she held tightly between her fingers as she turned my ear. She would ask me a question—I knew it was a question only because her wordless voice rose—and then pause for an answer, and I'd nod and smile and finally insist that I had to go. As I walked away I could feel her eyes at my back. Her name was Mrs. Robbins, and I liked her; she struck me as a funny old woman, and I appreciated the comfortable emptiness of her company.

One midnight when I couldn't sleep I let myself out and went down the stairs to the black ground, then crept to a clearing behind the building, between the back wall and the fence that separated it from Mrs. Robbins' house. I would have stared at the sky but the trees overhung the ground and I couldn't see, so I shinnied up the side of the building, passing from window frame to roof beam and then up onto the roof itself, where I could sit on the pitched tiles and watch the night sky. Mrs. Robbins' dog, a huge German shepherd with yellow eyes that were caked with unwashed sleep, came to the fence below, and together we sat there and listened to the breeze through the oaks. There was no moon, so I thought I'd serenade the stars, and this was the song that I sang:

If I don't get to sleep tonight
I'll lie awake instead,
And ask the lonely summer sky
Into my lonely bed.

As I repeated the verse and began a chorus I heard the old dog below me: first he whined, then he keened, then he tipped his head back on his throat and began to howl, and together we harmonized, from ground and rooftop. When my throat became so sore that my voice cracked and I couldn't keep the tune, I applauded the animal, got back down again, let myself into my room, and immediately fell asleep.

The work I had was hard, and I slept well most nights, but once a week or so I'd find myself hopelessly awake, and I'd get up from my bed, leave my apartment, and climb the roof. As soon as I had reached the peak I'd look down and find Mrs. Robbins' dog waiting by the fence with his tongue hanging from his slavering mouth, and we would sing. In time our book grew into a makeshift and varied thing. There were songs to woo the sheriff's daughter and bad-luck ballads, gun battles, ghosts, and lovers' leaps. I would beat out the rhythm on the shingles, and get to my feet and bow to the neighborhood when we were done.

One night we drew old Mrs. Robbins out her back door. The sky was cloudy and the moon was hidden, so I didn't have light enough to see her as she made her way tentatively across her back lawn, and my ears rang from my own voice, so I didn't hear her when she first called out curiously. I'd just paused between verse and chorus when she called again, and I immediately shut my mouth. But I'd forgotten which woman was deaf and which blind: I stood up on the rooftop and made a gesture to shoo the dog away, showing myself in the light of the moon. Her eyes met mine for a moment—and the dog started barking and then ran at his mistress and began to circle her, howling and showing his teeth. She put her hand to her chest and screamed, stepped backwards quickly, and then planted her feet, threw up her hands, and said—Glory! as I slid down the tiles and hastened down a drainpipe on the far side of the garage. By the time I reached the ground she was scurrying towards her house, and I heard one last, embattled Ooh! as her back door shut behind her.

The following morning was wet; a shower just before dawn had kindly watered the begonias in the backyard and left a small shallow puddle in an ear-shaped indentation in the driveway. I could hear my landlady coming, hear the knock of her shoes on the wood, and then the double rap of her hand on my door. When I opened it I found her standing there, her glasses perched on her nose, two fingers from her right hand gently stroking the frame. Her voice quavered slightly as she spoke, and she was so quiet that I'm still not sure of the story she gave me—her nephew, his bad chest, the damp air, a favor for her sister. Between clauses she glanced up quickly to see my expression, but I could think of none to wear. She was asking me to leave, and rather than let her finish her painful story I held my hand up to interrupt her, shrugged, tried to smile, and told her I'd be out in two days.

There was no singing either that night or the night after; it was bed and boredom, and by the time the sun came up on the second morning I'd packed my bag, put it in the trunk, eased the car out of the driveway, and was gone.

9

I had twenty-four dollars in bills and another two in change, and a week and a half to wait before my next payday; so I had no choice. The following morning I drove to work with my suitcase still in the trunk, and for the next few nights I parked my car in a riverside lot behind a highway restaurant about twenty miles out of town and arranged myself as comfortably as I could in the backseat. It was cold outside, and no matter how many layers of clothing I wore I couldn't keep warm enough to sleep well, so I lay awake for hours and watched the dark trees through the windshield, and between them, among them, the lazy river, the brown, loggy river, with its animal coils and heavy flow, and tortured myself with a ditty I learned in nursery school, a rhythm for spelling its name, with its improbable yips and hisses: MIS-SIS-SIPPI. I couldn't shake it; it stuck in my dry mouth like crumbs from a soda cracker even when, at last, I slept.

When morning came I'd wake before my little alarm clock had a chance to sound, peer out the clerestory behind me, taste my salty lips, and brace myself for another day. In the cold tile bathroom of a gas station a mile from Turner's parking lot I'd splash water on my face, and I'd swallow a cup of bitter coffee from a convenience store along the way. Eight hard hours later there was nowhere for me to go but back to the parking lot.

10

I've tried to write these, my confessions, many times, and each time I've stopped no farther than a few impoverished pages in, collected like so many useless pennies in a cup; and here I am, with a full fifty done. Will the book end so soon? Will our strange and powerful child now slink home, his ragged tail between his legs? No. Everything that I have promised will pass, or I am endlessly nothing.

The Mansion on the Hill

1

Oh, it's true I'm a magician. My mother was a witch, a Sycorax of the North Plains. When she left, she left me occult powers: I can conjure action at a distance, I can bring about the past, I can see around corners. I make accidents, and I can take them back. I put the stars in the sky, and I hung the moon among them; and I can move it at my will. I had no home, so I created one out of wishes and purpose.

It was a little past noon on a Thursday. I'd just finished clearing out the area around the Millers' fish pond and I'd stopped to wipe the sweat from my purblind eyes. It had been a long and tiring morning, and I found myself leaning on the handle of my rake, staring across the shimmering lawn at the gazebo at the foot of the garden, suddenly trapped in one of those dreamy moments when one's senses fix on a single spot while one's concentration evaporates into rare, alcoholic fumes. A brilliant red oriole—an omen I will always owe—darted across the scene, and when I blinked and broke my reverie I noticed the structure for the first time.

A few stairs led up to a hardwood floor that was elevated about four feet above the ground. There was a white painted rail around it and a semicircle of benches at its outer edge, with armrests that were worked up into pillars wound with yellow jasper, supporting a steep-sided roof. Behind it the Millers' property ended in a strip of trees, and beyond them there was another road; it had been placed so far from the house that it had no view to speak of. But it was a welcome little thing to me, because as I looked at it the point of its being gradually came into view. It was a forgotten folly, the generous whimsy of some past estate. I couldn't have known what had happened there once upon a time, a first kiss, say, or a late summer dinner, or tears from a runaway child; I couldn't have known how many days had passed since someone had last considered it. But I knew I could live beneath it peacefully, and if I could, I would. Anywhere I hang myself is home.

2

The rest of the day, spent tying saplings to stakes, passed so slowly that at one point early in the afternoon I thought it might have stopped, as if the sun had been rigged to a watch that had wound down. The evening crept along, my untasted dinner was endless, the time afterwards was a desert without dunes. I drove around for a while; I parked by the river, walked up the levee, and watched the dark barges glide by in the night. I counted the shivering pins of light on the far side. Then I got out and went down to the bank, crouched down in the tall grass, and found stones to throw out into the water, listening for the faraway lunk as they broke through the surface and sank. The sky was clear, the moon half full. The car steered like dirigible as I made my way back to the house.

There was a loose spot in the rusted fence and I wriggled under it and crawled on my hands and knees through the underbrush, pushing my pack ahead of me until I reached the edge of the grounds. There I paused, waited . . ... In the distance the dark house sat, strangely diminished, a shack under an enormous spiral projection of stars. The grounds were dark with gloom; it hung in patches in the air like morbid bunting. The trees were shivering in the breeze, the breeze smelled like sugar blossoms, and I could hear the high surrounding rasp of cicadas. A single light stared from a first-floor window. I raised a tentative foot and wondered. I could: who is more mooncalf than me?

The ground was spongy under my first step. With my second I trod on my breath and broke it in two; I left one half on the ground behind me and took up the other, and slowly tracked across the strip of lawn that separated me from the structure, with my back bent to make myself small. When I reached the base I tugged at a part of the lower fence until it came away in my hands . . . peered into the dark space . . . did, no, did something behind me move? I dropped down to a crouch and squeezed through the fence posts. The air inside was dank and mossy, and I could feel the crust of dirt beneath my splayed fingers. I pulled myself in, turned, and immediately shut out the pearl-grey light and the shadows of the yard by pulling the section back into its exact place.

Inside it was cool, damp, and quiet, and so completely enclosed that I could feel the dark pressing against my fingertips when I put my hands up. I couldn't stand upright, but I could get to my feet, provided I stayed low on my legs, and I could move around freely. For a few minutes I followed the edge of the enclosing wall in a waddle, stopping here and there to feel for the right spot to make my bed, and when I'd settled on the proper place I unpacked my bag of things, stacked my clothes carefully in one corner, and put my book on the ground beside them. Then I lay down on the hard ground with my empty pack beneath my head and waited.

My ears rang from the silence. Ninety-nine, ninety-eight, ninety-seven, ninety-six . . . my eyes stopped searching. Nowhere. A minute went by. A blue black day. A month of Sundays. And then with a sudden rush the room sprang open into the world, expanding until it became the world, a dark and unbounded globe that marked the limit of my possible life, a universal night in which I might meander, perfectly invisible, an invisible night, an unmoving giant in whose cavernous mouth I was soon asleep.

3

I was very comfortable that first thick night. I slept so soundly that my dream (I was the stage manager for an opera cast with orangutans) took in the ringing of my alarm clock (a warning that it was almost curtain time), and I was late for work. By the time I got to Turner's it was almost noon and the place was almost empty. I wandered down the cool, dark corridor, listening to the rhythm of my own footsteps and thinking of my new home; I was as spellbound and woozy as a lover on the morning after.

I found the dispatcher in the waiting room, frowning over some papers in piles on his desk. When he looked up and saw me standing in front of him he raised his hand and silently waved me away, accidentally knocking over half a cup of cold coffee with his paw. I waited while he bent down awkwardly to retrieve the mug, and when he stood up again he looked at me impatiently. Go on, go on, take the day off, he said. We'll make it up later.

So I went to town, where I mingled with the housewives saying hello to the shopkeepers and the men sunning their skins on the bench before the bank. In the hardware store I bought a little tin camping light and a few wool blankets, and then I stopped at the stationer's for a dozen sheets of black construction paper and a roll of tape. After I dropped the things off in the trunk of my car, I headed to the supermarket for some food and bottles of water. Along the way I counted the elm trees planted in little fence-squares at the edge of the sidewalk and began to write a song out loud, starting and stopping and searching my head for rhymes. As I passed an alleyway I noticed a figure loitering in the shadows of a loading dock—and just as I stepped up on the far curb he called my name—I recognized the voice as one I'd heard before, but I couldn't say where or when. I stopped and turned back.

He stood dead still in the shadow of a supporting post, did Jones; he waited patiently while I made my way down the block to him. As I neared him I noticed that his shoes were scraps and his clothes were rags, and not even the bright sun shining on the immaculate town could make him more than a wretch. He greeted me by waving a little and came up with a kind of pleasantly surprised smile. You found this place? he asked, as if it was a secret town full of legendary pleasures, an El Dorado of unspoken qualities.

I've been here about a month and a half.

Found work?

Gardening.

You'll like it here, he said. A refrigerator truck turned into the bottom of the alley and started up towards us, bouncing on the ruts in the road. It passed noisily, and when it reached the corner of the main road it stopped at the sign, and then headed off around the corner. Gardening. Fine, he said when it had disappeared. Then he patted me on the shoulder, turned, and began down the street in the direction from which the truck had come. He was limping slightly, as if his feet hurt, and as I followed him with my gaze I imagined him having shuffled across cornfields and grasslands, over hillsides and through woods, a mile at a time, tracing a long, unlikely longitude line that intersected with my own path at just that spot, fixed, in that town.

4

I spent the rest of the day sitting in the town library, looking at engravings of gardens, and when it was dark I went back to the Millers' grounds, let myself in under the gazebo, and went to work on my shelter. The paper went up to cover the gaps in the grillwork, and then I lit the lamp. The floor was scattered with debris, a few pieces of wood that a careless workman had left there, along with a single empty beer bottle and a sodden yellow newspaper. A woman's black leather shoe lay unreasonably in one corner. In no time at all I'd cleared them to one side of the space, and when I was finished I swept the floor with a piece of cardboard, carefully bagged the trash, and set it inside the door. With my housework done I blew out my lamp and lay down for the second night.

5

The first pair of men who worked the garden with me made an early, dramatic exit, and I never had a chance to get to know them. Even their names are lost to me now, though I still remember a thirtyish man with a fortyish face, and a strange and unconscious habit of asking me to repeat everything I said to him, and then finishing the second sentence for me. One afternoon they had an argument in Turner's parking lot about a ten-dollar loan that one—I don't know which—had made to the other. Words turned to insults, and insults to blows; they were pulled apart by a passerby. Then the debtor went to his car, took a small handgun from the glove compartment, and chased the lender towards the warehouse. Just as the latter reached the front door a bullet caught him in the backside. The sun was just setting in the western sky; at the sound of the shot a bunch of birds in a tree started screaming. The victim crawled inside and lay there moaning. The shooter sat on the curb outside and wept until the police came.

I'd already gone home for the day, but I noticed the bloodstain on the floor the next morning, and the dispatcher called me into his cubicle so that he could relate the story to me in close quarters. Gave him another asshole, he said, his face creased in ugly amusement. When the cops came they just laughed and handcuffed him. They came around here again this morning; turns out he jumped bail in Michigan a few months ago. He rested his hand on my shoulder, raised his furry eyebrows, and guffawed until tears came. Hell. Anyway, he said, giving my forearm a warning squeeze, you're in charge of the Millers'. There are two fellows waiting outside; they'll be working with you now.

The first was a boy about my age whose maker had cemented his bones together with sticky wit, and had given him little more to hang on them. He didn't mind much; he said his name was Spot, and there seemed to be nothing that he minded much, and I who minded everything envied him just a little. The second was an older man, a small fellow called Baker, who was quiet and gruff to the point of sullenness. By noon of that day his face was the color of burning anthracite from a combination of the midmorning heat and the contents of a small, tin flask that he kept in his side pocket, and later that afternoon I found him napping beneath the shade of a tree, his hands folded across his belly, his face, with its half-open mouth and half-knitted brow, made stupid by sleep. I gently woke him and put him to work again, though not without having to ignore his grumbles. Well, I could ignore them: there was so much to do, a patch of ground that needed to be pampered into giving up its colors, a hedge that needed clipping, fat bags of smelly fertilizer to be spread among the roses. The garden as we got it was pretty enough, but it had nothing on my manhood dreams, which climbed like ivy and opened like irises, and if I had to muscle them out of the ground, I would. I thought the three of us were a team, however unlikely—a winning hand, three jacks in hearts, clubs, and spades spread beneath a king and queen who remained face down and of unknown suit, at least until the bet was finally called and the accounting began.

6

Late one breezy Sunday evening I settled onto my mattress to read by the low light of my lamp. I'd spent the afternoon window-shopping in town and had picked up a bag of ripe cherries from a grocer's before I drove back home. As I lay on my back with the book propped on my abdomen I was popping them one by one into my mouth, depositing stem and pit into the palm of my hand and then transferring them to a small pile on the ground beside me. By then I'd come to see the garden as mine—I was its keeper, and it was my front yard—but the book distracted me as well; if I hadn't been so caught up in the familiar pleasures of its pages, and so careful not to mark them with pale pink juice, I might have heard my neighbors coming, but I felt as isolated as a man in his manor, and it wasn't until I heard the muffled sound of a pair of footsteps on the stairs outside that I was drawn from the words to the world. In a hurry I put out the light and sat as quietly as I could.

In time the sound of a girl's voice drifted down through the floorboards, but I couldn't make out the words, only a mash of syllables and squeezed vowels that went on for some time, evenly cadenced and blunt, as if she were reciting a story that she'd practiced for days. In some places she was emphatic, in others amused, in still others resigned, but her voice never rose or fell by as much as a fourth. Eventually she wound down, started up again abruptly, and then stopped. Another voice appeared, again a girl, but softer, more patient, and slightly drawling . . ... The first answered briefly, and with a note of assent. I heard a fit of coughing, which I used as cover to get to my knees. Then there was quiet for a time, the trembling of proximate thoughts, and light footsteps leaving.

I did follow them. I couldn't resist it, though I swear I tried; I sat on my hands, I pressed my ankles together and rocked back and forth, I squeezed my eyes shut until shards of ingrown light impressed themselves on the black of my lids. But as the two girls strolled slowly across the grounds back to the house I found myself slipping from my shelter and following their voices, and while I lost them among the azalea bushes, still I kept on, pulling shadows over me as I moved towards the great house. There were lights on in a first-floor window, and I saw figures darting across the facade of the house and then swiftly disappearing just before the back door banged shut. A few moments later I came onto the cold deck out back, and I got down to my knees and crawled behind a wicker chair to peer through the window into the golden glow of the living room.

There were four. An oldish, portly man with a neat grey beard sat in a deep black leather chair in the center of the room, with a large book open and face down on his lap and an unlit pipe pressed between his lips. His wife, a fine-featured woman with her hair pulled back, sat on a couch that faced him, one arm lying along the back. Beside her sat her eldest daughter, half-reclined on the cushions with her legs drawn up underneath her to make room for her little sister, who sat on the floor before them with her head resting against the seat behind her. The two girls were still flushed from their trip through the garden.

Father was speaking softly—the pipe wiggled in his mouth until he reached up and removed it. I crawled a little closer to the window, hoping I might hear a little talk, but I felt light on my back, and I scurried back into the darkness. By the time I was hidden again he'd finished. He put the pipe back into his mouth, tipped his head back with the satisfied look of a man who's just put out a small, harmless fire, and folded his pink hands across his stomach. His wife reached down and gently stroked little sister's long brown hair, and little sister shifted her luxurious lap on the floor and pursed her lips into a cherry red pout. Her mother gave her a tender glance and murmured a word or two to her. Her father brought his head up again and spoke a sentence out loud; big sister sighed, bent her head back and lowered her eyelids, shook the hair off her forehead, and opened her hands on her lap. She spoke some words of whatever mark to the ceiling; it was the same voice I'd heard from within my cave. Mother arched her eyebrows in lazy surprise, and little sister turned her head, but not far enough to see the other. (Pause.) All resumed their original positions. It was the entire cast, full stage and floodlit. I wasn't bored; I waited there and watched until one by one they shook their evening off and started upstairs to bed, leaving me to myself.

Late that night I lay awake in my hiding place, nursing circus visions, dreams of flight, and terrible, longing cramps. Lights burn bright in Hollywood; in New York couples cut across avenue traffic; children play evening games in Dallas yards. Saturday night beckons like a distant bonfire. Surrender for a moment, will you, to my misery, and sing along to whatever tune you like:

Who is this who spies my home?
What worm is it that turns the loam?
As green a boy as ever was
Monster is as monster does.

7

House warm, proud house, with a chimney on the roof and a Wilson in the yard. By noon the next day they were all gone, and under the guise of detaching a green cellophane garden hose from a spigot by the back door I stole over to the kitchen window, cupped my hands around an invisible pair of binoculars, and pressed my nose against the dark glass to see what I could see. The room inside was ringed with a gleaming white countertop and equipped with a number of mysterious appliances. The ceiling fan spun slowly above a black-lacquered wood table, on which someone had left a still life of a fruit bowl and a half-empty honey jar. A tap on my shoulder made me jerk and spin around: it was Baker, standing behind me with a pair of gardening gloves in his right hand, very carefully not smiling. The thing is out of gas, he said solemnly, and then he stuck the tip of his index finger in his ear and gently waggled it.

Well, go on and get some more, I replied, trying hard to seem annoyed.

I need the keys to the truck, he said, and slowly held out his hand.

I drew them from my pocket and gave them over to him, and he disappeared around the side of the house. A moment later I heard the engine start up, and he was gone, though the thing must have needed some rare and special thingly fuel, because he didn't come back for an hour and a half.

That night, and every night after, I sneaked in from the back road and relaxed for an hour or so in the comfort of my gazebo, and then as the moon came up I stepped out into the cool, sylvan setting of the grounds and made my way towards the house. From behind the car in the driveway I could see into the kitchen, and there was a convenient pair of bushes behind me that I could scamper to if anyone came out to run an errand. I could watch the living room from the deck, and the dining room from a spot within some brambles at the far side of the house. In fact, with all the house's windows I had views of most of the first floor, though at odd and unscheduled hours I'd hear piano music coming from one room into which, because it faced the front and had no sheltering bushes, I could never see.

What was I watching? A boy is not a spy, and I had no thought of trying to catch them at something secret. But I was endlessly engaged by the details of their daily lives, the cupboards full of dishes, the rituals before bedtime, the receipts saved in a drawer in a desk. I wanted to see the Millers in their banal balance, to see how rich and routine, how stubbornly real their habits were. One wouldn't push a spade into the ground to find surprises, only to open a book of natural evidence, to discover that it's natural and to know it as such. And I have no taste for sordid fruit or blackmail.

What I know of what happened in that house I first learned by watching. Later words were whispered to me in the heat under humid night covers, but by then I had eyes other than my own to see with; in the early months of that summer I was an audience of one, and I had a passion for figuring that sustained me in my unique appreciation. I loved to follow my hosts as they made their home, which I imagined dug out of my rude and wild garden, and by the time May had begun and the earliest buds had bloomed I'd learned enough about them to feel a sort of flush of good feeling whenever I found them again.

The old man was a lawyer, and from the size of the house and the luxury they lived in he was a successful one; and he had a lawyer's temperament and a lawyer's walk, contemptuous, slow and literal. His name was Holiday, and his wife was called Anne. Big sister had a year left in a private school called Trinity a few miles away, and her name was Marian. Olivia was the youngest, separated from her sister by a year and a half, and she attended the same school.

Marian was a fond, sore, and impatient girl; she saved her troubled affections in a painted lockbox on her dresser top, and spent her time in minutes. What she did with herself I don't know—I almost never saw her—but I was always aware of the fact that she wasn't there, because I knew from the night I first saw her that she was the most clearly tempered of them all, and therefore the one least susceptible to me and my appetite for belief. So she was my ghost, and I was hers. Still, I knew she wouldn't be there for very long—she'd leave for college in another year—whereas I intended to be there forever.

So there was no hurry. Anyway, Olivia was in no hurry. She was the quiet one, and when she moved she swung on her hips as lazily as a porch swing in the summer heat; her fingers trailed on the tables as they passed; her clothes were always slightly frayed or awry somehow. She would lie languidly on the couch, her cupid mouth slightly open as she read a novel, occasionally rubbing the tip of her nose slowly with the back of her hand; she would sit in the kitchen late in the afternoon and watch her mother cook, dropped down in the seat so that her legs extended across the linoleum floor and her chin was pressed into her chest. Anne would come to her with a bowl to stir or a carrot to cut, and Olivia would slowly pull herself up, turn to the kitchen table, brush her long brown curls back, and set about her task with a look of perfectly absent concentration on her face, her head tilted slightly to one side as she watched her hands work.

There she is again, yawning, stretching on the back porch one Saturday morning, her shirt raised on the soft, pale isthmus of her stomach as her arms strain behind her head; or coming up the walk from school, her brown eyes half closed against the afternoon sun; or alone in town just before dinnertime, waiting at a traffic light with her bicycle. And there she goes, leaving me hiding, doped.

8

In time I decked out my crawl space with trinkets and toys. I bought a rug and I placed it on the floor, and some pieces of wood made a sort of low table and stool to sit on. Empty crates pilfered from the garbage pile behind Turner's served as a dresser without drawers, and from my occasional trips into town I gradually acquired whatever things accumulate in a house, magazines and a pair of sunglasses, a pillow, pens and pencils, a set of tableware, a second chair for an imaginary houseguest, a waste-basket, and a second lamp—this one battery-powered, because I worried about fires.

It was a warm and wet spring that year, and while I was snug at night, I still had work to do during the day, and it was often interrupted by rain. At the first sign of cloud cover, Spot, Baker, and I would retreat to the eaves of the mansion, where we'd wait and listen to the water drop around us. The dampness would remind me of Olivia, filled as it was with mixed and inviting notes, and I'd smile to myself and count the shivers in my attention. When the rain ended we'd step off the patio and resume our work in the garden, and within a few minutes the sun would begin to show in the sky, less as the familiar liquid yellow pool than as a brightening source in one corner, still occluded by clouds; I would spy the noble frame of my gazebo down the hill and make a note to pick up something or other on my way home from work. A butterfly would flutter by. Then, as the bumblebees began to buzz loudly in the heat, I'd wander the wet acres, while water dripped down the fat, full veins of the green leaves around me; my shoes would soak through, and then the cuffs of my pants, as my garden passed beneath my padding feet.

Baker would glare at me whenever I asked him to take up a shovel again, and then walk as slowly as possible towards the spot I'd pointed out, stopping every few steps to hitch up his pants, or to blow his nose into a rag that he kept in his front pants pocket, or to light one of the cigarettes that, no matter how many times I asked, I couldn't keep him from stamping out in the grass. Spot, on the other hand, just said, Done, boss, lowered his eyes, and smiled to himself— somewhat mysteriously, I thought, as if it was all, ridiculous as it may have seemed, exactly as he had predicted.

When we were finished for the day we'd drop the truck off and check our tools into our lockers, and once, when Spot and I were walking slowly back through the silent parking lot, he invited me to join him for a beer. The sun was low in the sky, and the air was warm and hazy with golden pollen. He stopped for a moment, placed his hands at the base of his back, and stretched his spine. A little pin-ball maybe, he said. Maybe chase some, you know . . .. He laughed shortly, and I watched his Adam's apple travel an inch up his throat and then drop back down again.

What about Baker? I asked.

Hell no, he replied, looking around to make sure we were alone. God. Come on, you have a car, right? I nodded. Then let's go.

I wanted to head back home, to take in the last hour of fragrant daylight before the sun went down, but he followed me to my car as if I'd already agreed. As I unlocked the door on the driver's side he rested his arm on the hood, peered through the window at the dark interior, and said, Nice. How much was it? I told him and he shook his head. Got to get one of these, he said.

The car glided to the gate. Where to? he asked.

I don't know, I said. I could feel his eyes on me as I spoke.

There's this bar . . .. He pointed left with one long finger.

With Spot providing delayed directions—Left here, back there, he said as we passed a boulevard, and I braked so suddenly that a bottle on the floor of the backseat bounced up against the gearbox and broke—we came to a dark wooden building at the back of a grey gravel parking lot, a mile or two past a decrepit racetrack in the fallow fields north of town. Inside there were a dozen or so tables, extending back into the dim recesses of the room, but only one of them was taken. Three boys and one girl sat there, less another girl who had left a half full glass of beer while she used the pay phone by the bathrooms; I could see her small, dark form against the rear wall, one hand flat against the top of the coin box while she held the receiver to her ear with the other.

I had never been in a barroom before, and I was still standing in the doorway, staring at the rows of dusty pharmacy glass behind the counter and thinking how similar it all was to the bars in books and movies—though I hadn't expected the sour smell of stale beer—when Spot took a stool and motioned me to the one beside him. The bartender brought us two dark brown bottles and then turned back to watch a basketball game on the television above the old refrigerator at the far end. You're not from around here, Spot said speculatively. Nope, you're from another land, far, far away—another world, where, um, trees grow upside down, and, and women give birth to ponies.

I laughed. Nebraska, I said.

Of course. One of these days . . . he shook his head and raised his bottle to his lips. What? What?

One of these days what?

He looked back over his shoulder to the table by the telephone.

He scratched the side of his soft nose. See this? he said, flattening the point above his nostrils against his face. No bone. No bone at all, boss. I got it broke so many times they just took it out. Anyway . . . Look at that, and he nodded his head towards the table. Should have stayed in school, don't you think?

The girl on the phone had finished talking and was making her way back to the table, her eyes mnemonically glancing down and to one side while she bit contemplatively at one corner of her lower lip. In her dark clothes, and with her hair arranged so that the parted side was tucked behind one ear while the other half fell over her eyes, it took me a moment to recognize her. It was the gesture she made as she took her seat that tipped me off, the way she opened her hands, palms up, as if she expected her friends to hand her answers. I've got to go, she said resignedly. My mom wants me home for dinner. She stood up again, jammed her hand into the pocket of her jeans, and came up with a few bills, which she dropped like trash in the middle of the table. Close. Where is her sister? Somewhere.

No bone at all, Spot said again, looking carefully at Marian as she pulled on a grey sweatshirt, several sizes too big, with the word Trinity written in purple across the chest. A girl sitting with her back to me said something that made her laugh and nod her head as she lingered over leaving. Finally she raised her hand in an absent good-bye and started for the door. Nope. I turned back and watched the girl through the mirror behind the bar. She paused in the doorway so that her eyes could adjust from the cool shadows of the bar to the glare outside, and then with a sun-wet shiver she disappeared through the door like a swimmer into a clear summer sea. Spot turned back to me and drummed briefly on the bartop with his fingers, a tattoo that gradually faded. He turned his bottle around in his hands and then peeled off a corner of the label. At length he said, I guess I'd better go too, boss. He lapsed into a parody of his own open accent: I'm plumb tuckered out. Besides, my mom wants me home so she can remind me that I'm . . . a disgrace.

I'm buying, he said, and put a five-dollar bill on the bar. You're driving.

On the way to his house he asked me to stop for a moment at a convenience store. I watched through the window as he pointed to a rack behind the cashier's back, but I didn't see what he'd bought until we were back on the road. Look at this, he said, and pulled a magazine out of a brown paper sack. A police car passed. I glanced down just as he flipped it open to a picture of a young woman on all fours on a bed, naked but for her crimson high-heeled shoes, a pair of thigh-high crimson stockings, and a string of pearls that hung down to the bedcovers. She was kneeling away from the camera's eye, with her head turned up so that her bleached blond curls fell down her shoulder blades. Her back was arched, and her legs were parted to reveal the damp, dark, enfolded cleft where they met, and with the long fingers of one hand she was gently gripping herself. Her skin had an unnatural texture, and I noticed that her toes were slightly spread, as if the film had caught her just as her efforts were being wrung out to the last, eccentric border of her body. It made me think of a butter truck overturned on a highway, but Spot was gazing at it as I turned my eyes back to the road, and for the rest of the ride he flipped through the pages, pausing now and again to compliment an image that he admired.

9

Within a few weeks the blossoms began to bud, and by the middle of May the grounds were composed of pages of opening leaves, operatic folios and quartos. Wine ran through the earthly spine, and honey dripped from the fat stamens of the plants. As the air warmed, scents appeared like notes on a staff, monster clef, in the key of me.

That land was my first medium, and as I practiced it I grew more adept at judging myself; I saw its resistance and my own response, measured my powers and met my personality. In making my gift I made myself, in colors more vivid than I brought to the piece. I soon became so absorbed in the green work of gardening that I would sneak from under the gazebo after midnight and do a little digging, a little weeding, a little planting; but never mind, I made the landscape open itself up. I don't know where my talents came from, unless it was simply desire, but there they were, and my monsterpiece grew greater with every day that passed. I was a Demiurge, filling the world with the reluctant stuff of creation, the something that I made out of nothing, by casting it away from the dull silence before its existence. Passing the herb garden set my nostrils to quivering, and the hedges were full and deep green; when I walked among them I was embarrassed, the way some women are embarrassed by the lusciousness of their own bodies (Olivia, in a pair of shorts, looking down at her thighs as she sat on the kitchen counter and quickly hopping down again). The water in the pond became sweet and clear, the soil was damp and brown, and every blade trembled in the dolorous sunlight, each one complementing the next, until their individual shades and spears mingled in a humid expanse, a blanket so soft and heavy that it trapped every sound, and apart from the occasional song of birds and the noiseless hum of flourishing, the garden was silent.

These are notes of a long transformation, compressed by necessity: I find it almost impossible to account for the individual days that made it up—not because I've forgotten, but because in retrospect their qualities have been rewritten. They flash by like the jerky cinema stories of a flip book: three characters make their way in from the gutter where the pages are bound, stopping once or twice and bending to make some vague motions on the ground. We don't look at one another. Drops of cartoon sweat appear on Baker's forehead; he abruptly wipes them away with the palm of his hand. An awkwardly flapping bird crosses above us, then a tiny dot appears in one corner, a point that gradually expands, swells, its details becoming clearer: it's a whole planet, with rivers and valleys, and as it grows it overwhelms the scene, filling the sky. Spot disappears under its shadow, and then Baker, leaving me alone to stare up from the garden as a city materializes on its surface, a street in the city, a house, and in the backyard the accelerating image of a girl in jeans and a striped T-shirt, who waves to me from the sky, her ground, as she swoops down on me—and then the last page unexpectedly flaps through my fingers, and the book falls to the floor.

10

One Thursday evening I found the house glowing with soft gold, and through the windows I could see Holiday and Anne bustling about as if on the distant stage set of some amateur parlor drama. Then she crossed to the left and sat down at the kitchen table to write out a long note, and he went up to their bedroom and began to draw clothes out of his closet and dresser. In time she followed him upstairs and disappeared into their bathroom, and he began to pack a large suitcase that lay open on their bed. When he was finished he stood it neatly by the door, then went down to his desk and began to put papers into his briefcase. They were going away.

At first I balked at the thought, since I was afraid that I'd be lonesome with the family gone. But neither of the sisters moved: while their parents packed they sat and watched television, and when the suitcases had been placed by the front door Marian patiently received a final word, kissed her mother good night, and saw them to the car. From some foliage at the side of their property I watched as their ember-red taillights floated down the hill to the street and then disappeared.

The note was a set of instructions, but I never did have a chance to read it. While her sister watched uncomfortably, Marian set fire to it over the stove three minutes after they'd gone—and the two of them jumped identically when it suddenly flared in the pan, leaving a black smudge of soot on the ceiling that no one but me ever noticed. For the rest of the evening they sat in the kitchen, talking over a bottle of their father's red wine, until Olivia grew so tired that she could barely hold herself up, and she went to sleep.

Her sister moved to the couch in the living room, turned out the light, and lay alone with the television, stretched back against the cushions with her eyes lowered, her hand pressed between her closed thighs. The minutes didn't change, but the girl herself gradually became glassy and bare; and her nerves began to fire, tying urgent knots in a long, slow loop. Her hand moved, then she turned slightly and wriggled her hips a bit farther down the cushions. Her mouth opened slightly, and a few seconds later she pressed it tightly shut, as if to block her tongue . . . she was night fishing by lamplight, waiting, intent on a string in dark water, on an invisible jerk below the lapping waves. Her brow furrowed as if she was intensely curious about something, breathing.—Suddenly she winced, shivered once, and then twice more in quick succession, and then again, and then she relaxed back against the pillow and slowly let out her breath.

For a few moments she lay there, relieved, motionless in her daydream, and then she sat up slowly and glanced around the room. It was still there, so she went to the front door and locked it, turned out the lights, and walked swiftly, surely, upstairs to bed.

I was still asleep the next morning when the two sisters left for town, but I was awake by the time they returned, with the back of their mother's car filled with grocery sacks, and I was wide-eyed as I watched what they unpacked: bags of cookies and chips, dips, pretzels, and all kinds of fruit—grapes, apples and oranges, peaches—and two cartons of cigarettes and a bag of stacked plastic cups, and several large containers of juice and coffee-colored soda, and so many bottles of beer and liquor that I was stunned—was that what a parent prevented?—until I realized that they were going to have a party. They'd planned it for the next night, a Saturday.

That evening I lay awake with jitters, my head filled with unruly plans that stood in a ragged line at impatient attention, while I inspected and then dismissed them, one by one; and when they'd fallen away I found only one that remained in place, standing unsteadily under nervous clouds on the parade grounds. It was necessary because it was possible, and possible because it was left. The sheer momentum of the act's modality pricked me to it; I never would have been so brave.

11

The following day brought the first truly hot weather of the year. The dew had dissolved by mid-morning and the air grew heavier as it warmed; by noon it had turned to steam, and as I sat beneath the gazebo, reading the morning paper in a diamond of light that came through a hole in the floorboards above, drops of sweat fell from my forehead and mottled the newsprint, and my shirt became pasted to my back. A local church bell struck twice and then quit, as if it had just managed to compress a pair of brass droplets from the summer sky before retreating back into the darkness of its tower, exhausted.

At three in the afternoon two girls with bright yellow hair appeared out of the brilliant sunshine, coming up the drive in a bright yellow car; a little later a boy with a bicycle arrived, propped the thing up against a tree and untucked the ankles of his pants from his socks, and then came through the front door without ringing the bell. In the cool, hazy darkness inside the house I could see Olivia moving about in a polka-dot summer dress, her calves and the plump white flesh of her upper arms exposed. She stopped and touched her bare neck to remind herself of something, and then started again. The plants needed to be watered, and she padded into the kitchen, emerged again a few moments later with a long-nosed green plastic watering can, and started over to a cactus by the back window.

Marian was leaning forward on the couch, with her arms crossed over her crossed legs. She gave a faint, wilted wave as their friends entered stage right and collapsed into chairs, and her friends didn't respond at all. Olivia finished her chore and lowered herself next to her sister with her pretty feet up on the coffee table. I could see black ovals of dirt on her soles. She wriggled her toes and sighed. After half an hour she and one of the girls began to get ready; they unbagged the food and put it out on a table in the living room. Afterwards the five of them sat in the dining room lazily sipping iced tea.

Then Olivia and the bicycle boy disappeared in a car. When they returned a half an hour later they had two or three bags of ice, which they emptied into a tin bucket from the basement, and the bucket, in turn, went into the refrigerator. There was nothing left then but the waiting. For several hours they sat, as their boredom and impatience grew. The television talked on endlessly, applause, laughter. They tapped restlessly on the armrests of the couch, they checked the bathroom one more time . . . and then it was nine. It was ten-thirty before the first guests arrived.

By eleven there were a dozen in the house, and by eleven-thirty two dozen. I went back to the gazebo and changed into the only clean shirt and pants I had. Numb hands, not mine, let me out of my bedroom. The yard was very quiet, and the steps I took were long and bouncy; they settled slowly, like a balloon, while I thought—not thought, exactly, but dazed and dozed, and listened to nothing as I thoughtlessly crossed the shadowy lawn. Then I stole down the side of the house and sidled up the front path to the door, attaching myself to a group of a half dozen other boys, taller than me and older than the sisters. They were completely unimpressed with the preciousness of their position, but more I can't say; not a feature or gesture remains. I remember only that they were laughing easily at something that I, my head filled with damp fog, had missed. When Marian opened the door she greeted each one with a kiss on the cheek while I held back in the shadows and then, just before the door shut, pushed my way in—Oh, sorry, she said, as she tried to shut the door on my shoe. She wouldn't give me a second look or a third word for the rest of the night; she left me standing on the threshold, the living room open before me, while I gazed into the noise and the featureless faces.

12

Was I nervous? I was. Was I afraid I'd be exposed? Of course. Was I monstrously self-conscious? Yes. Did anyone approach me? One did. And who was it?

13

She caught my eye in a mirror that hung above the couch in the living room. I was standing against the far wall, with a small, empty plastic cup in my hands. I was watching their friends; I wanted to box them all together in order to have a little container full of rivals. The glass shone against the wall like a window onto another room, and through the crowd I saw Olivia's profile reflected, one cheek framed with rococo curls of chestnut hair showing as she faced me across the room. She'd changed her clothes, and the soft grey man's shirt she now wore was so large that, untucked, it fell almost to her knees. I watched her watch me for a few moments, watched her glamorous blush in the glass. When I shifted nervously she fixed the angle and frowned, glanced over again, and silently laughed as she realized I was watching her reflection. She turned towards the mirror and I could see her eyes on me, and then she was obscured; the room had become so crowded that it was only through the figures of her friends that I glimpsed her open gaze, once, twice, gone, and a third time again. You're crazy, no way, someone said. It can't be more than about eighty. A boy in a red windbreaker was nodding vigorously at his sandy-haired friend.

She came carelessly towards me, without effort or thought; she didn't look at me again, and I suddenly wasn't sure if she'd seen me at all, or if she had some other reason to move so. She raised her hand briefly to touch a girl's shoulder in greeting as she passed, and smiled distantly. It's a hundred twenty something. This is before he went to Oakland. I swear, I know, I lost a bet on this. I felt slightly sick. The tape player howled with music, over which a man sang in a low, lazy voice: Sometimes I don't thrill you. Sometimes I think I'll kill you. Just don't let me fuck up, will you. 'Cause when I need a friend it's still you. What a mess. The lights were too bright in the room, the music was too loud, and it felt like a cell, a noisy, frantic capsule falling swiftly through time and the quiet darkness outside, turning over and over again. I wondered how the furniture stayed in place, why we weren't tumbling onto one another like dolls in a box. A tall girl with long brown hair turned to the wall, tipped her head back, and swallowed something small, a piece of candy or a pill, or a bug. Sandy-hair was gesturing violently as he shouted at his friend, and still she made her way towards me, raising her eyes to mine as she neared, slowed, and stopped by my side. My features turned to soft clay.

My name's Olivia, she said, and she held out her small hand and smiled as if at some secret joke. I felt the warm pads of her palm touch mine. What's your name? she asked, as if she'd known once and just needed to be reminded. Wilson, I hissed, my tongue a flopping fish in my mouth.

She laughed. What's your first name?

Wilson, I said. I could hear my own voice: it was wrong.

56

She shook her head as if to clear it, and laughed brightly again; I saw a sweet pink kiss flash past. Well, Wilson Wilson, she said.

I hope you're enjoying yourself. You're not drinking anything; can I get you something to drink? There was a slapback echo on her voice, a ringing around her words that lingered in my ears. Sweeter than wine. No, thank you.

So, she said abruptly, aiming her eyes at mine for a moment and then turning them away. You know Marian, right? Have we met before?

I don't think so. (I'm a goblin that lives like an ornament in your garden, a garden I made for your family.)

. . . .

I was invited here by a friend, but I don't think he's shown up yet. I said: I'm sorry.

She smiled shyly, hugged herself gently, and twisted a bit on her feet as if she were dancing to some music; she stretched in her skin, she bit her plump ruby underlip. She tucked an errant curl behind her pink ear and I saw the tiny glitter of a diamond-drop resting in her lobe. She moved like a girl on holiday in her own prettiness. Don't be, she said. I'm glad you could come. She glanced up and waved to a boy who'd just come through the door, then looked at me again with her eyes wide. Don't be sorry, I mean. I hope you'll stay.

(I'll stay for months, for years. I have nowhere else to go; this is my green island.) Actually, I think I'm leaving now, I said.

No, stay. Do you know why a whale is like a picket fence? Let me go get you something to drink. She became mock stern and waggled a finger at me. Don't you move, I want to talk to you.

All right, I said. She turned away and headed towards the kitchen, and when she was out of sight I pushed my way through the room and let myself out the back door, and as the funhouse echoes faded behind me I slipped quietly away, a shadow on the back patio, a scape, a goat in the garden, a poltergeist with a knocking heart sprawled on a thin mattress under the gazebo.

14

Congratulations, climbing vine; and to you, black beetle, on the opening of your pale, iridescent wings; and to you, Wilson, on having made such a fine occasion, a celebration: little sister, with her affections, her liquid moods and long lashes, her cinema faces, had risen in my mind like a full moon above the Atlantic:

What did you learn this palace spring?
When you are queen I will be king.

15

Two days later Anne and Holiday returned from their trip to a spotless house (less one crystal drinking glass, now slivers and shards in an outdoor garbage can), a pair of daughters with no particular news to tell, and a boy still hiding in their backyard.

I know my desire for Olivia's company will seem like a terrible decision to some. The chorus is already restless, gossiping, worrying, predicting a bad moon, terrors, a broken tower. Good players, we'll let it pass. Olivia knows, I know, that as much as I chose I was chosen. I admit it was bad, but not because she or I was bad: it's just bad to be. Anyway, this is not a case of beauty consorting with beastliness; for if I'm not handsome, neither am I entirely impossible to look at, and as a child I received my share of favors. I have an afternoon preserved in my memory like a chip of ruby glass in a box, when a youngish widow visiting my father's office touched my cheek as she was leaving, then brushed my hair back and left a quick kiss of lipstick wax on my lips, and an invisible cloud of perfume about my head. My father saw, and when she'd gone, with an icy flash of her jewels and a bright smile that lingered in the waiting room for a few moments after the door closed behind her, he took me into his examination room, sat me in his chair, and paced the floor in silence while my reddened ears rang with what was left of her laughter. Finally he stopped, turned to me, and said, Be courteous, and remember what you are. I do remember, and the woman's compliment means nothing to me now—it makes up for nothing.

16

Where were you then?

Hiding.

Hiding?

I was in the garden, you know. I was afraid.

Oh, no. You didn't have to be. Come here, put your head here.

There wasn't much else I could do. I didn't have anything to give you, so I don't know.

(Smiles.) You're so serious sometimes. You, mmm, I love this, the way your hair, goes . . .

Suppose I'd just come to the door one day and asked for you.

Asked who?

Whoever answered. If it was you, just asked to see you.

I'd have been flattered. And then what?

I don't know. How does this go? A movie, or, what do I say?

A walk.

A walk?

A gentleman comes calling, if a gentleman comes he asks a lady out for a stroll, if the weather's nice.

If it isn't?

Then he comes back.

17

The next Monday was a school holiday. Holiday went off to work that morning, leaving room in the driveway for our now clutch-sick, lurching green truck, but both Marian and Olivia were in and out all day. I was trimming a hedge in the back of the house when I heard their mother's car start, and then late in the morning the sound of the two of them calling to each other came across the great lawn, but I was careful to keep hidden. I made myself invisible: it's one of the things I can do.

That afternoon barefoot Olivia emerged on the back porch, wearing blue jeans and a loose white T-shirt and carrying a pitcher of iced tea that her mother had made for us. From the fish pond I saw her wave once, her arm tracing a wide, awkward arc over her head, and I turned my face away and sent Spot up to thank her. A minute later I glanced up to see him stop on the flagstones, smile, and start towards her, and I watched with agonized frustration as he spoke to her, one hip slightly bent as he rested easily on his feet. For a moment I saw my dreams drive up to the edge of a cliff, but she politely answered whatever comment he'd made and then turned back into the house. I only went for my own cool and bitter glass, with its sun yellow slice of sour lemon and its shiny cubes knocking together like my knees, when I was sure she was inside the house. No luck? I said to Spot as he passed me on his way back into the humid garden. No nothing, he said, without looking up. I couldn't help but laugh with relief, an outburst of chattering and indiscreet glee that rankled him. Fuck you, too, he said, and left me there with a cold face.

18

A drop of water hangs from a wrought-iron rail, quivers and glitters with captured light, a shining globule trembling with the tension of its own tiny gravity. Beside it another drop appears, and then a third, this one excruciatingly bright from the newly emergent sun. The first drop hangs, falls in a vanishing quicksilver streak, and another one replaces it.

A brief gust of wind rustles the trees, and a moment later they shake loose a sudden, late epilogue of secondary rain, a sort of softer playlet about the downpour that's just ended, and Holiday, who has come out onto the back porch, and whom I've been watching from the rose garden, a pair of pruning shears frozen half-open in my hand, feels a hundred unexpected drops striking his shoulders, lowers his head, and hurries back into the house.

19

According to the notes that I have kept in the soft sentences of my undying memory, the next morning was clear and dry. When I awoke, stuck my head out of the back of my gazebo and peered blinkingly up at the sky, I found that someone had painted a cloud in one corner, but it had disappeared by the time I arrived at work, and the day promised to be perfect. I took my place on the end of the bench and waited, but an hour passed and the dispatcher forgot to call my name: Baker and Spot were sent to the house, my house, with another man I'd never seen before, a fat, bejowled beast with tiny eyes. His name, I learned when I overheard Baker introducing him to Spot, was Willie. When everyone was gone, the dispatcher called me over and told me that I was wanted in the office. There the manager sat, behind a long table covered with slips and papers. Without asking me to sit, without meeting my eyes, he began to speak.

Gardening is a cooperative thing, he said. Everyone's personality has to be, what's the word . . . everyone has to get along for everything to work, so the client will be satisfied. We provide a service; that's what we're paid for. You've been a promising worker, he said, and you're a bright boy. We were happy with your work, and we thought you'd do well around here (with the unhappy tense my smile slipped to the floor). But Mr. Miller came down here yesterday and complained for an hour. So we sent a supervisor out this morning, and he came back with . . . well Jesus, it's a fucking jungle over there, it's a wilderness, it's—are you doing any work at all? I started with astonishment and opened my mouth, but he looked up for the first time from the stack of invoices on his table, and with a wave of his hand he silenced me. There was a pair of oversized red plastic dice on his desk, and he picked them up and began idly trying to match the dots. So it's been decided that you aren't working out. He set the dice back down again: boxcars. He was sorry. He thought for a moment and his face changed, as if he had been struck with a sudden sincerity. You are a strange one, he said, as if I wasn't there at all. Strange.

I paused to allow my blood to settle, and when the roiling in my ears had faded I got up from my seat, smiled to show my teeth, turned abruptly, and walked out the door. I could find other work; but the garden was mine and always would be.

20

It was particularly warm that night, and because it had rained in the evening the grass was wet and the smell of undergrowth drifted through the meshwork of my walls. As it grew dark I rose from my bed, opened my door, and peered out at the garden. That afternoon we'd mown the back lawn, and the air was thick with the sweet smell of cut and rotting grass. It was a cloudless night, and the stars circled above me in dizzying whirls, spotted bands of white in the darkness. In the time it takes to tune a guitar I had my clothes off and had begun a kind of unemployment dance. I trailed my hand along a row of buds; I scratched my bare back against the rough trunk of a tree; I somersaulted down a small slope; I wriggled my toes in the dirt of a flower bed; from the herb garden I picked sprigs of mint, crushed the leaves between my fingers, and rubbed my flesh until it stung with the sweet oils. I picked berries from the bushes, popped them into my mouth, and spit their skins onto the ground. I tore up a handful of grass, reveling in the ripping sound it made and scattering the blades onto the crown of my head until they mixed with my hair and fell onto my face. Am I alone? I asked myself. Yes, I am. The whole house is sleeping, the whole world is sleeping, and I'm all alone again. But I am the Genius of the Place.

I loped over to the fish pond with a weed stalk between my teeth and found my own familiar reflection in the black glass. Wilson,

Wilson, he called you a strange one, I said. I reached into the water to stir it until my features distorted and dissolved, and then I jumped through the ripples with a giant splash. Ooze sucked at my toes when I touched bottom; weeds wrapped round my feet when I launched myself over to the other side. When I got out, dripping wet and shivering in the starlight, I shook myself like a soaked dog and turned towards my home. It was going to rain.

I could see a yellow flickering in the darkness; it lay like a slick of phosphorescent fluid on the ripples in the black water, and when I looked behind me I found tiny licks of light on the far windows of the house. With dark clouds in chase I hurried across the bottom of the grounds in a crouch, pulling branches over me as I stopped behind trees, pressed my cheek against the bark, and looked around. What's that smell, what fine burning grain in the air? Hot smoke: I was almost at the light before I realized it was a fire at the foot of my gazebo. I could see the door to my crawl space propped up against the bottom of the structure; there was a man outlined against it, an adipose figure who stood tossing dark objects into a small crowd of flurrying flames. As I watched he paused and looked around him, and I saw his face clearly, with its expression of permanent contempt. Behind him I could make out the dark outline of my chair, the slats on its back bowing like ribs behind translucent leaves of fire. Next to go were my clothes, and then a box that had contained an envelope with a month's worth of savings in it, now money gone to smoke. Then he bent down and took hold of my rug by one corner, and with a motion like a bullfighter turning a satin cape he raised it up and brought it to settle over the flames. A plume of black smoke and orange sparks flew into the air, and for a second I thought he might have smothered the flames; but then the edges of the cloth began to flicker, the flickering widened towards the middle, and the whole thing went up like some giant, light-giving flower, the brightest bloom in the garden, with petals of fire that mocked me with the work of my undoing.

I stopped myself from crying out by biting my lip until the skin split and my mouth filled with the thick taste of my own blood. Holiday paused, puffed on his pipe, watched the fire. After a moment he crouched down in the darkness, and when he rose again he was holding my book; and as the fire with its brass band cadence suddenly grew again he balanced its weight in his hand, bent his head until his glasses caught the firelight, and flipped the pages . . . paused at a plate, frowned, and then casually tossed it into the flames.

The old man stood there until the fire was finished, kicking at the ashes to be sure there weren't any embers left, and then he glanced once around the garden and started back for the house. As soon as he passed me I started running towards the gazebo in hopes of saving something, but it was too late: I could see as soon as I arrived that while the fire had died, my last poor things were ashes, mixed with the charred and blackened logs that he'd used as fuel.

As I hid and crouched that endless night, covered with a crust of dirt and salt, I thought about the meanness of my weather. All I'd wanted was to make nature in peace, I said to myself. No, I don't know how the world was made, and what's more, I don't know why. I don't know why I was made it in it, and made to make it back: I could hazard fifty guesses, and get fifty cuffs for my troubles, fifty insults, and five hundred lies. Holiday stood for Holiday, and stood behind every one.

If he'd taken my job from me, but left me my shelter, I would have been content. If he'd evicted me from my shelter, but left me my things, I would have been content. Even if he'd set my things on fire, but left me to work freely in the garden, I would have been content. But he left me nothing, and at last my fury descended upon me in a flock of winged w's, like birds before their sharp beaks nip into flesh: if it was a war he wanted, well, I would wage my own, and begin it by singing.

Some say men were given tongues to praise whatever heaven they admire, but I have mine to curse my enemies, and lungs to blow the insults on them. I howled until I was hoarse. This was my song:

What is a man? What does he know?
He's a coward, a bully, vulgar, low
A fool with a vain and tempted eye

Fickle clouds in a summer sky
Greedy, sullen, pompous, mean
Feeble, dull, a mere machine.

And what, instead, can we say of me?
What purpose do I fail to see?
I'm proud and gentle, brave and just,
So full of desire that I'm going to bust,
Dispensing my uncommon joy.
Light a candle for the boy.

What employment could I desire, now, beyond the pursuit of my future?

Stranger in the House

1

Self-portraiture is a kind of folly, like trying to grasp the fingers of your right hand in the same fist. The sky on which we write our constellations is not a mirror, since once hung the stars shine by their own fire, and while the course we plot assumes that they're fixed we'd never know if they wandered. It's true nonetheless: I was born over my senses, and I was a very difficult birth. I struggled with all of my tiny might. We all know that there's no comfort or calm equal to the dark solitude before birthdays, but that wasn't why I was reluctant to be born: I didn't want to be at all, and I fought for hours, for days, to keep away from the world. Having been born, and now having lived, I sometimes think it would have been best if I'd used the moment of my first gasp to go right out again, but I was instantly impressed by the smart light of the delivery room, the shining metal tables and floors, the beeping of the instruments, and I reached my pink hand out towards the masked features of some doctor or nurse, and couldn't turn back.

I can see my father standing in the hospital hallway waiting for the news: I was the news. I can imagine him watching impassively as the nurse brought my soft, swaddled self up to the glass so he could get a look at me. Sir, a boy. He was a strict and quiet man, my father, a man with an incalculable and unexpectedly clear soul, which was absorbed by his work like well water in a dry flower bed. That day fulfilled one of those ironies of generation, of being born and begetting, that warp stories into sacredness: my grandfather was both a doctor and a tyrant, a tough and difficult man, so my father was scrupulously principled; he thought of himself as a name under a moral law that he sustained only by correcting himself through the years as a man corrects a dray, using his own doubt as a bridle and his capacity for shame as a bit. I was the third issue, and he would bear it without complaining, as if an otherwise absent providence had determined it. I don't know what grief he might have kept alive over the years, but I'll ask you to believe that his life from then on was an attempt to concentrate, as if to sharpen away the brute moment of my being under the small abrasions of his duties. For a long time he had studied deserving, the way a foot soldier studies war, and he'd taught himself to see everything: he stood in the bright hallway, his thoughts carefully hidden: he simply watched, and slowly nodded.

And there in my imagination is my mother, damp, pale, exhausted, and relieved, lying in a hospital bed with her hair unpinned and cast out on the white pillow. My father is in a chair beside her, waiting anxiously for her first look at the son she delivered. He holds her hand. A knock comes at the door, she turns her head expectantly, the nurse pushes her way into the room with her arms full of clothes, and there I lie, quietly covering my face with my tiny hands.

About a year later my mother died in an accident—I see an airplane landing in a rainstorm, though I don't know why—leaving me with my father. All that remained of her was her signature in the front of the poetry books that were sorted on one shelf in my father's study, an old-fashioned signature made in fading blue ink by practiced penmanship; and there were three photographs in which she appeared—one on my father's desk, the second on the mantle above the fireplace, and the third, which I saw only once, in his wallet. I was unconsciously young when she entered heaven, as my father, in a lapse from his usual plain-speaking, put it, so I have no memories of her at all. I have no suit against her. I don't know what kind of woman she was, and I never asked, since it seemed to be the last thing my father could have answered; I was afraid he'd turn as brittle as old paper, and then dissolve into dust under such a bright light.

2

My parents had moved to Lincoln just before I was born, to a blue frame house on the edge of town. It was huge and hollow inside, with a front hall laid with black and white diamond-shaped tiles that I used to slide over in my stockinged feet until the soles of my socks were grey with dust. Towards the side there was a porch which was seldom used, because it was cold in the winter, and the winters were long. My bedroom was at the start of a long second-floor hallway, and my father's was at the opposite end. He and my mother had bought the place expecting to fill it with children—there was a bedroom for each of four—but his sense of a house died with her, and he simply left the unused rooms empty; there was a single rickety chest of drawers pushed against the wall of one, a rolled-up carpet laid against the baseboard of the next, an unplugged lamp on the floor of the third. Absurd, but I think he was also a little sentimental, so we never did move.

I used the rooms as a diving bell. I wasn't happy, and as a boy I liked to imagine a sea in place of the Great Plains, with a hole in the bottom where I could live, passing midnight days among the translucent ferns, the shells and silt. In school one afternoon they pulled the shades and showed us films from diving ships, dark flickers of what they found near the boiling springs as far below as a man could go: giant white worms, fat mushrooms, flathead fish and eels. They did nothing but swim the currents and feed. I didn't even know how they went about making more of themselves, but I knew I wanted to live with them, because I knew that I belonged to nature, too—and why not? Freaks and sports of all kinds are hers to make and keep, spiny fish, moss and mung on trees, mandibles and hammered features, and choking smoke from fires, and crawling dirt, and brackish water, and me. If my father was bothered he never showed it. We lived together, he and I, in a house that was far too big for us alone, and in which half the rooms had furniture the way months have full moons.

Like him, I can now grant that nature's insults aren't insults; but when I was a child I reckon I made things hard for him. From my bedroom I could imagine him, after one of my wildcat tantrums, returning to his study to sit silently in his chair, his head lowered into thoughts of his gone wife and my improbable unhappiness. I know he found it difficult and bewildering. At the bare blank and diminishing end, now, I'm grateful to him for his generosity. My dear father, small town doctor with a spook for a son, a boy who made fears.

3

Daddy never brought stories of his patients home; their sufferings were secrets, and he took the privilege of his invitation into the systems that sustained them very seriously. But my curiosity about the patterns of disease was insatiable, and like a wind chime it could be set trembling and ringing by the slightest move. I used to watch him carefully while we sat at the dinner table, looking for some sign he might show of the travels of his adversaries; if he sighed softly just as he lay his fork across his plate at the end of his meal, I'd imagine that a patient had worsened during the night before; if he lingered over a forkful of potatoes, I decided that a new possibility had just come to him, and the next day would bring brisk arrangements; if he fixed himself an extra cup of coffee after dessert, I guessed that he was rewarding himself for having effected a cure—unless he added an extra spoonful of sugar to it, in which case I could tell that he was expecting to study late into the night.

When he did have work left ahead of him he used to take the kitchen table to pore over the illustrated journals that arrived regularly in the mail, looking for a new therapeutic treatment, or something to suggest that a diagnosis might have been off. As I passed from the empty living room to the empty dining room I'd see him, his grey head bent over his wonderful research while the illnesses of men and women all around the world formed swirling, page-bound currents of blood and compounds. The magazines he read would be open to their difficult maps, the charts of deep waters and undertows that some anonymous second had prepared and published. He watched them all like some quiet, latter-day Poseidon, with his favorites and battles, redirecting Furies and tides to achieve his ends, the health and completion of the men and women who came to him with their aches, their breathing troubles, their messy cavities and miseries, their numb limbs, their sleepless, bedridden bodies.

I remember leafing through his books from time to time; I used to sneak into his library when I came home from school and choose from the leather-bound medical volumes that lined the shelves. Had I had the proper temperament I might have learned something, but I never thought to wonder how the things they described might have had a place in the causal order. I wasn't born to be a doctor; I'd rather think of the singular, the particular, the actual, than spend time making real sense of the general world of symptoms, or cures. I used to look at the pictures and try to imagine the body that had posed for them, and then recite passages aloud for the rattle of the syllables, without knowing or caring what they meant.

One fine day I came across a pathology textbook, as devoted to viscera as a slaughterhouse. It began with a special inset: on the end paper there was a pair of skeletons, like exotic musical instruments, half violin, half vibraphone—though one, with its deep, curving centerplate, looked as if it would be much richer and more resonant than the other. Over them successive transparencies could be laid, thin plastic sheets on which were printed, first the shaggy skein of nerves, then the fatty organs, then the tubules of blood (red with oxygen, blue as a drowned child), then the fibrous muscles, and then translucent, pale pink skin, until a whole and very patient couple finally appeared, standing like sentinels over the carnival inside. I read through the book with the devotion of an initiate, skipping over the technical terms that seemed to multiply as the pages made their way towards the distorted glimmers and gazes, the pulp and sordid perfume that lead to the blots of flesh from which you and I, in our several ways, began; but I always returned to the frontispiece, and I never tired of assembling that map, with all its clever, interlocking layers.

I wrote stories of my own, in a notebook that still sits in the bedroom desk drawer where I hid it. It was a school composition book, bound fat with a strip of black tape over the spine, and the lines on the pages were wide enough for a child's hand like mine to keep its characters under control. The cover was a painterly abstraction, black ink spotted over a white background until the individual flecks melted together, making a sort of camouflage pattern; in the center a space was cleared for my name and home address, an oasis that I, inclined towards invisibility even then, left uninhabited. Inside I carefully wrote out little tales about a wild, illiterate, and helplessly destructive Wilson; I hid in swamps, in ship's holds, in other people's houses, where I stole daughters and murdered fathers; I ate insects and stray, misfortunate men, and when I was done I belched loudly, bent down, and beat the ground with my fists until the trees shook in Africa.

For every empire, even of a child's limpid imagination, there is an emperor, and I liked to imagine the great day when I was crowned. There would be a hall so huge that I wouldn't be able to see the ceiling. The light would come from rows of flaming, smoking torches that hung on the walls. At one end I would stand, boyish and unembarrassed, raised on a platform and gazing out with a slight smile over an assembled mob of monsters. They'd groan their cheers, they'd stamp their stumps on the ground, they'd shake their staffs in the air, and I would be declared President for Life.

4

Lincoln in those days was a small, quiet city under a huge blue sky. It wore the smell of the fields that surrounded it the way a farmer's wife wears a cotton dress, and like a farmer's wife it was bare-legged underneath. Within a few blocks of the main street the houses fell down to two-story frames as if on their knees before the sublime beauty of the Plains: there was so little substance to the whole, from limit to limit, that if the University and the Capitol hadn't held it down like nails I think it would have become detached from the earth and floated silently up into the sky, leaving me alone at last and unwatched in the dirt below.

Our house was on the south side, and our nearest neighbor was the Widow Foster. She had always been the Widow Foster, and had always lived there, but in all the years we lived next door I never did meet her; I seldom so much as saw her in the open air. Still, on afternoons when I played lordly games in our yard I'd occasionally catch a dark glimpse of a serpentine form behind the windows of the French doors that led to her porch, and I'd seen the shadow of her figure often enough to know that she was a pleasant-looking old woman, with white hair and a white throat and a body as bent as a bicycle after an accident. All services were delivered to her door, and we grew used to the sight of a grocery delivery boy or florist standing at the top of her front stairs, waiting patiently for her to make her way up from the back of the house. Then one day when I was eleven, under the spell of one of my father's funereal afternoons, I first contemplated the mysteries of mortality, using our neighbor as an example. I never even left my room: I just wondered, and the next day a man with a package rang and rang, paused, rang some more, peered through a window, and then came over to our house and spoke to my father for a moment. I was sitting in the kitchen when he came to the phone, and I watched as his index finger drew the dial in a circle. I remember asking myself what law had been suspended to reduce the familiar seven digits, with their inconsistent rhythm (a measure that waltzed, a measure that marched) to a brief and urgent three.

In the Widow's place came a family from Kansas City, a young couple somehow connected to the University. I spied on them from my window as soon as the enormous green and yellow moving truck pulled up to the curb in front of their door. For the rest of the day the movers carried their furniture into the house, while a girl in a grass-stained dress played among their legs, sat sullenly on the front steps, poked around their new backyard, and finally turned her pale moon face up to my window, where she saw me standing and, after looking around to make sure no one was watching, slowly waved.

Her name was Liz, and she was a tomboy, pony blond and always into something. Aside from the day she moved in next door I never saw her wear anything but blue jeans. She smelled like hay and grape juice, and she had downy sunburned skin and long, thin limbs, and a habit of standing with her mouth open and dazedly blinking whenever she came across something that excited her. For reasons I'll never understand, she befriended me with a wide, sly smile one weekend afternoon just after they'd arrived. I was on my way to the corner mailbox with a stack of my father's letters, and she stopped me from the edge of her lawn, came down to the sidewalk, and asked me if

I knew how to make a knot that no one could undo. When I said I didn't she sat me on the curb and showed me, using my own shoe-laces and then laughing shamelessly as I struggled in vain to get them untied again. We finally had to cut them apart with a pair of sewing shears she borrowed from her mother.

For the weeks that followed we used to meet on the playground at school, sit side by side against the jungle gym, and eat lunch while she watched me with glittering eyes, then meet again at the end of the day to walk the few blocks home, where I'd leave her at the side-walk and watch her as she dashed up the stairs to her front door. Then one winter's day she brought me into her house instead, and while her mother fixed dinner in the kitchen she led me down into her basement playroom, and under the matter-of-fact fluorescent light she simply disrobed and showed me, with perfect grace, in what besides her long hair our differences lay, as if she were the end paper of my favorite book come to life. I was silent through the entire event, I was so fas-cinated by that form, with its *trecento* shape and coloration, at once elegant, devout, and awkward. I still remember the soft, smooth tex-ture and smell of her bare skin, already stippled with delicate goose pimples from the cold, the way it was gathered about her bones, the slight sharp taste of her breath on my face as she moved towards me and gently kissed my burning cheek. I couldn't have imagined that anything had the power to be so entirely naked, to be so present in its plainness: she was the first thing I'd ever encountered that depended upon nothing else to exist, either in itself or in my mind, and as the sun dwindled down at the horizon, unmoving, the afternoon stopped dead; and she suddenly grew serious, backed away, and said, okay, now it's your turn. When all at once I realized that she was looking at me as I was looking at her, I spooked and shook my head No, and when she tried to cajole me and reached her hand out towards a button I ran away, hightailing it up the stairs and through the kitchen, past her mother's astonished stare and out the back door. When I reached my own room, breathless and with my heart backfiring, I lay face down on my bed and dizzily replayed the moments I'd just passed, until my father came home from work and called me down to dinner.

What did you do today? he asked as we sat down at the table, and I, thinking he already knew somehow, lowered my head, reddened, and then to his astonishment blurted out everything. His awkward, nonplussed silence when I'd finished only confused me more: he shuffled the beans on his plate with a fork, cleared his throat, swallowed half a glass of water, and then changed the subject.

5

Liz drifted away on an uneasy tide, waving good-bye just once and half-heartedly from the foot of a long path that I invented and put in place of our own all too real driveway, just as, the week before, I'd removed our house from its neighborhood and put it in a green clearing in some dark, medieval woods. Afterwards she ignored me when I passed by her and her friends as they played hopscotch on the sidewalk in front of her house, and school, which for a few weeks had been almost a pleasure, again became a miserable duty, the more so since the princess had willingly gone to some unnameable dragon.

I remember very little of my teachers, with the exception of one young woman, fresh out of college and no match for me, who asked me to stand before the class and recite a patriotic poem we were all supposed to have memorized the night before. I refused at first, but she insisted, so I stood, stared at the ceiling, and repeated as much as I could remember, changing the word country to monkey throughout. The boys in the back row giggled, and her face as she scolded me remains clear to this day. Little monster, she said, and I left the room on a brief, imaginary trip to an island in the Mediterranean, where I quickly wrecked a passing ship.

The others have faded into a pale, multiform band, within which I can make out single features, a beetle brow, a bald spot, a chalk smudge, a hand holding a lesson plan, but not one complete person; they have become blurred into a dim audience, frowning at a failing act without seeing that failing was my act. See, the old books lie. Teaching Caliban to curse made him Caliban. And Huck is one part

Tom, and Tom is two parts Becky, and we are all three parts runaway Jim. So I did a lot that others thought I'd do, and I did it because they thought I would; they were the spectators at my coming to be, and I was a master, a monster, of finding and finishing their expectations, the doctor's strange son, who seldom looked at a man directly, and never at a woman, who slouched and hid and whose voice was always quiet. As every local reviewer knows, the logic of character is so appealing.

Still, I suffered from the typical torment that children pay one another. My classmates' boos and catcalls were the never-ending music of my adolescence. It's so predictable that it hardly bears recounting; someone always gets it, and I was the one. Instead let me draw a picture of my own closing credit. It was the first example of my artistry, my way with nature and my powers.

It was a late spring day, sunny and breezy, and they were standing in a circle around me in the schoolyard during lunch hour, burying me with their usual insults. I was waiting expressionless at the center of the ring, and I was prepared to stand there and play the object of their scorn until recess ended, as I did each time some secret signal rang and they gathered around me. But on that day, as I stood and listened to the rising, hurdy-gurdy sound, a single syllable from a single voice—I don't know whose—suddenly appeared from out of the ring and, like a cold chisel, knocked at just the right spot to split my temper open, so that my fury spilled out: I opened my mouth and emanated ill will. I made fun of one's unkempt clothes, another's fat father, a third's disgusting lisp, and when I could think of nothing to holler at the next in line I simply invented a failing—and when the failings ran out I received a gift of tongues, and a flood of mean energy, and I began to rage and rave at their blank faces, cursing them with a might that grew inside me, stretching my skin until I was sky high, one thousand feet tall, bitter all the way up and so angry that the weather changed: the sky darkened and I shouted up a North wind; papers, notebooks, textbooks swirled at my feet, the trees bent almost to the ground, my hair whipped across my face; on the other side of the playground a line of bicycles in a rack collapsed with a soft clatter. Through my squinting eyes I could see a teacher coming out the back door of the school, with her skirt tearing across her legs. She stopped in her steps and watched on, transfixed by the impression I made, as the wind blew and I leaned back with my arms outstretched and howled commandments to the elements.

I don't think any one of them understood half of what I said, but they were so taken aback by what I'd done that one by one they backed away, as if in the face of a supernatural force. Only Liz stayed on: she was standing by the fence that separated the playground from the street, hanging on with one hand to a diamond-shaped link while her red jacket flapped in the storm and her blue eyes opened wide in a look of astonished, delighted admiration. When the rest turned and ran I was left alone with her, and I let the wind subside. I remember that it was very quiet afterwards.

Liz let go of the fence and gazed at me with solemn curiosity.— Then she began to clap her hands together, and as the girl's childish, single applause drifted across the pavement I raised my arms, called down a rainstorm, and walked all the way home in it. I wasn't bothered again.

6

Something mean hangs high over whatever law is made, what-ever comfort a good man commands. To worst and best alike nature comes, in best and worst fashion. So I was made a sport, and my father was made with a weak blood vessel behind the wall of one temple.

One cold winter day it broke and he died. It was a Monday, and he'd gone home for lunch; a cancellation early in the afternoon left him free for an extra hour, and anyway he had left a file that he needed on the desk in his study. He was fixing himself a sandwich in the kitchen when all of a sudden he felt faint, his breath came short, and his ears rang, so he shuffled up the stairs to his bedroom, lay down on top of his bed, closed his eyes, and there and then he left.

I was brought out of civics class that afternoon by the school nurse, a usually chatty woman who silently monitored the passing tiles on the floor as we made our way to the principal's office. Am I in trouble? I asked. No, no, she said, and put her cool hand gently on the back of my neck. I'm sorry, child. She sniffled and sighed; I had no idea why.

I was ushered through the anteroom—they were all watching me—and into the principal's office, and he put aside his papers, took off his glasses, and told me that I'd been called home from school. Then he rose from behind his desk and walked me to the empty street outside, where a colleague of my father's named Cooper was waiting, dressed in the curiously old-fashioned manner that he preferred; under his coat he wore a white shirt, a string tie, and black pants. His ankle-high suede boots were wet with melted snow and streaked with grey from the street salt, and each had a shiny spot near the big toe where the leather had started to wear through. In one hand he held his hat; he put his other arm around my shoulder without speaking. I shrugged him off. As we walked to his car the snow squeaked under my shoes, and the wind was so sharp in my nostrils that I pulled the neck of my sweater up over my mouth and nose until I could smell my own sweet breath mixed in with the humid wool. Cooper's dark green sedan was in a cleaver-blade of sunlight at the edge of the parking lot, glinting against the muddy snow that had been piled up to the curb. We drove to the house in solemn silence, pulling gently into the driveway that my father and I had cleared the day before; I remember the sound of the engine ticking from the cold as we walked away from it, the dark house against the white edge of the rise in our backyard, the snow and blue sunlight. There were no shadows. I was fifteen years old. He was lying in his bed with his eyes closed, his rare soul having dissolved into the sky like the foggy vapors of my breath that afternoon. For a few minutes I was left alone with his body so that I could say good-bye, but I couldn't bring myself to utter anything at all to that wax effigy, and when the door opened again I was found sitting in a chair across the room, staring at the bed as if it were a macabre sideshow exhibition.

Cooper was assigned me for the next few years, and he was proud to have received my father's commission. He was a nice man, never married, a facile guardian: he gave me a room in his house to sleep in, and a meal or two a day, and after I'd rebuffed him a few times he stopped trying to draw me out of my obvious misery and left me alone. I was an easy charge, and since I intended to finish school and be gone as soon as I could, I never gave him a reason to try to be more. I wouldn't want to see him again.

My father had willed the house to me, and I insisted on leaving it more or less as it had been before he died, but I packed away his clothes and personal effects, and I donated the most useful of his medical things to a small, poor school nearby. The cutlery was worn, the silver dulled in spots from the years he held it, however gently, in his subtle hands, but he'd left a wish that I give it away. I put his books into storage and took his clothes to the Salvation Army; the furniture remained, along with the silent pictures on the walls and my own abandoned bedroom. I stopped by the house almost every day from then until the moment I left, although there was nothing for me to do there but sit in the living room and read the walls. On weekend nights when my classmates were at parties or cruising the main strip in their cars, at holidays when families gathered, on summer afternoons when girls went walking together and smiled at boys, I was alone in that dark house, too frightened to leave, waiting for my helpless youth to end.

One day during my last year of high school I decided it'd ended at last, and I walked out: that's all. That afternoon I visited Cooper in his office, stood before his desk, and told him I was gone. He fingered the frame of his glasses, nodded carefully, quizzically, and asked if there was anything he could do. I'd like for you to watch the house, I said. If you can, keep a little heat on to keep the pipes from freezing. He nodded again and promised me that he would. I dangled a set of silver keys over his papers, explained which fit where, and set them on the blotter before him, and he opened a side drawer and deposited them inside. There was nothing to say after that: he stood, shook my hand, and walked me to the door.

I left the next morning, wandering out into sky blue spacetime, footstep by footstep. Aside from the clothes on my back and in my suitcase, a day's food, and my toothbrush, I took only one thing when I left, a book of Daddy's, my favorite, the one Holiday had erased forever, the one in which I could make a couple appear and vanish again in neat, successive stages.

7

I've been a long time telling this, I know, but my name is not No One and I don't come from Nowhere, or Nod, or straight from a vague and perfunctory Nonage. I could have shouldered up a mountain and buried myself beneath it, or swum down to the Gulf, but I stayed in the Millers' garden, which was mine. You see, I thought I was supposed to be there. If not there, where? There was nowhere else in the world; I could see my future as clearly as saints see the heaven they covet, and for the same reason: I had read it from my past. So I moved in with them the next day.

It was a new day to them, an especially late part of the night before to me. On my hard knees, on my naked seat, open to the weather and soaked through my raw red skin, I'd shivered in a sleepless delirium and waited for the sun to rise, and then discovered that it doesn't; the grounds became as grey as a dove's wing, and then, as the sunlight burned off the folds of fog that appeared at the bottom of the garden, a morning blue gradually appeared, mixed with tinges of aching yellow reflected from the moisture at the edges of the leaves. But it was my bare and open eyes that finally made the world appear, that drew the forms of the mansion and its garden out of the darkness, and not a circling sun.

I waited through the endless early morning, drifting on the pale hours like a becalmed ship, and when they'd all left, Holiday to his office, Anne into town, and the girls off to school, I carefully crawled out from beneath a bush and sneaked towards the house, crouched down on my bare feet and shuffling across the pebbles in the driveway. There was a line of basement windows at my knees and I tested them all, but they were locked. So was the back door, and the ground-floor windows, in one of which I saw my own wild reflection, my arm rubbing my forehead for an idea like Aladdin rubbing his lamp. Next I scaled a tree to the second floor, but the window was out of reach, and in any case circumscribed by the silver tape of their alarm system; behind it was a cool, dark chamber with a soft bed and a delicate print of a riverside path among ancient yews on the wall. I searched the facade of the place for some way in that I might have missed, but it was sealed up tight. I'd been up all night and I was so tired, you know; I could barely get enough sense together to make a thought; it was like trying to strike something underwater. I sat there and stared at the impenetrable house, while around me the colors of the world drifted down like garments hung on a ghost.

A few dreamy wavering minutes passed. I scratched my abdomen. There was an air conditioner in a window above me, humming busily. It stopped suddenly as the thermostat sank past a switch, and the world stilled. I had just started to try to think again when I heard a noise at my feet, and before I could scramble up into the foliage a small, sharp-featured face appeared, gazing up from the basement to where I sat. Wilson? It was a second before I recognized the face, with its pale pink eyelids blinking in the sunlight. How are you? asked Jones. Why don't you come down here?

I slipped back down the trunk of the tree, chafing my thighs on the corrugated bark, and found him staring out from the basement, no smile on his face, no expression at all. He gestured with his hand. Come in, he said, and withdrew inside. The window slid shut, and I could see him through the dark glass, standing below me, staring up out of the darkness. In I went, crawling backwards over the casement and dropping down from the ledge onto the cool concrete floor. When my eyes adjusted I looked around, but my friend was gone; he wasn't behind the supporting post, or in the corner shadows, or hiding on the other side of the door, and I finally realized he'd left me again, and I let him go.

I'd come into a storage space lined with stacks of carefully labeled cardboard boxes. In the next room I found a boiler, and in the next a workspace lined with tools, with a staircase leading up to the kitchen. I chose the boiler room for my bed; it was already spring and I knew no one would be down to use it. I found an open box of musty blankets, and I stole a few and stuffed them behind the door until I needed them. Then I went looking for clothes and a little lunch. I was hungry and cold, and frightened, and I couldn't think.

Holiday was a fat man, where I was a skinny monster, not even fully grown yet, but I wanted his suit and went to find it. From the kitchen I wandered naked through the front hall, and naked up the carpeted stairs with the pile between my dirty toes. In the hallway I paused, bounced once on the balls of my feet, and entered the old man's room. It was so tidy, with his bed made, the drawers closed on his clothing, his bureau top bare.

Under the shower in his bathroom I shampooed my matted hair. I dried myself with a soft white towel and buried it at the bottom of the laundry bin, and I was careful to open the window so that the steam would clear, and to brush away the talcum powder that had fallen to the floor, a little dusty pool within which, like obverse islands in an archipelago, lay the small oval giveaway prints of my toes. Then I walked bare-assed into his bedroom and rummaged through the full closets until I found a suit that I admired; it was made of soft ash-grey wool, carefully tailored, beautifully cut and stitched; and when I thrust my hands in the pockets

I found a crumpled ten-dollar bill that the old man had forgotten, a prize slip of green paper. There was a blue-and black-striped tie hanging on a rack on the door, and a white cotton shirt in his drawer, still in the grey box from the dry cleaner and with its encircling paper band intact. As I stood uncovered in their bedroom I unwrapped it, shook out its soft folds, and buttoned it on; then I drew the suit off its hanger and shrugged it over my shoulders, and as I knotted the tie I sang this slow song:

> Oh, why don't you love me?
> Oh, why don't you care?
> Is it my clothes, dear?
> Is it my hair?

Is it the way that I creep up the stairs?
Oh, why don't you love me?
Oh, why don't you care?

My new clothes billowed and bagged all over; the waist of the pants fell to my bony hips; the sleeves of the jacket hung over my hands. In the full-length mirror on the backside of their door I looked myself up and down and waved my arms like some giant, mad crow trying to fly. I gave myself a cheerful smile, I winked at myself, and then I wandered off.

In the kitchen I found some leftovers in a covered dish in the refrigerator, a sort of chicken stew. I quickly finished it, rinsed the bowl and put it in the dishwasher. I found a pale yellow cheese in a drawer, which I placed in my right-hand pocket, and a box of pale yellow crackers in a cabinet, which I placed in my left, and then with my suit bulging I made my way down the back stairs just as the sound of a motor came up the driveway.

For a moment I pondered my unlikely reversal; there I was, inside looking out on the driveway, waiting for Anne and her daughters to come home and fill the house with sound, to come to me. Instead a truck pulled to the side of the house, with a country song playing on the cab radio. As the engine died the music stopped mid-chorus, but one young, tuneless voice continued singing a few more words: Her old man, he never liked me, so me and her ran to Tennessee. Over the state line, we . . . umm . . . preacher said, Do you? and I said, I do.

I could hear them talking to each other as they put down the back of the pickup and began to take down their tools. I wonder what he's doing now, said Spot. Baker made a spitting sound. Off bothering someone else. That kind always finds someone to bother. Together they lifted down a lawnmower and dropped it with a bang and clatter on the pavement. Baker laughed. Now maybe we can, get some, settle back some. Jesus Christ. I mean—here he grunted as he lifted a bag of fertilizer onto his shoulder—I don't mind working, but that boy had us running all over the goddamn place. Put, put this here, plant that thing there, dig that up. He leaned back on the bed of the truck, wiped the sweat from his forehead, pulled a can of beer from his pocket, and laughed again: I thought I was going to take a swing at him one of these days. Spot said Amen and wiped his forehead on his shirttail.

Inside the house I hung my head and shook it slowly from side to side and then retreated back into the darkness.

8

Holiday went back to the gazebo every so often to make sure that I hadn't come back; I used to see him wandering down to the end of the garden, poking around the bottom of the frame. It was a useless precaution, no harm to me, no good to him. I simply made my way in and out of the basement window every night.

He had given instructions to the manager at Turner's; he wanted the place trimmed back, and from the first day Baker, Spot, and Willie had obediently tried to lessen it. Flowers were pulled up, plants pruned down, vines stripped off walls and lattices. But I knew that everything depended on making it beautiful and keeping it made against the old man; it was unthinkable that I should leave the grounds to the three careless hirelings. The house was at the center of the garden, and I was at the center of the house, drawing the great, growing circle of land to my chin like an enormous, bedecked quilt. In the quiet of night I moved about, my bare hands serving as hoe and clipper, rake and spade. Without the bitter taste of wage work I fattened myself on my free labor and kept on. I'd ordered my passions into a first paradise, and I wanted to populate the place with my own subjects, with dwarfs and hermits, a carnival of mystery rites and delirium, voices calling back and forth across the divide between myself and the world I'd made; I wanted to grow something that knew me, and people the place with little Wilsons.

The trees grew new branches for me overnight, silent, gesturing limbs, here beckoning, here shrugging, or stopping imaginary traffic, or raising hallelujah arms, or tossing off an obscenity. The flower beds crept across the paths until they formed a natural maze, a king's conceit with a dozen false turns and dead ends. A fat, high shaft of shrubbery changed, at its own command, into an antic natural topiary, with a bulbous top and a pair of protruding balls at its base. A small sea of white mushrooms popped up in the center of the lawn; their heads were mown down, but by the next morning they'd reappeared.

Turner's crew never did discover why all their efforts to turn my gorgeous garden into a polite little backyard failed. Holiday's contempt couldn't dissuade me, and his violence couldn't cow me. I still stripped off my clothes and wandered out onto the lawns; I still marched with my knees high among the hedges; I still splashed boldly in the fountain after they'd all gone to bed; I still ran through the paths and across the lawns as fast as I could, my parts flapping in the breeze, and then I stopped and crouched, buck wicked and berserk in the darkness: I was the royal better of the land, a usurper. For the first time I no longer felt watched by the world, under the great dome of its everpresent eye.

It was the garden of my America, the one I'd found, the one I'd made, a sky that faces a sky, with our boundless airs, our inventions and our atrocities written on it like vapor trails. No one had to tell me it was right. Here was my world, the world of my book, the book of my life; here was a country made for mooncalves, as if at any crossroads I might meet another like me, headed in another direction to make another backyard, and we'd tip our hats at each other politely, grin like drifters, and move on. Yes sir, I've always known that somewhere else some other boy is having his day, but there are plenty of places for us to invent our sudden trials, plenty of room for us all—though only one who wrote this song:

I dug the ocean, I built the hills.
Should have my face on dollar bills.
I smoothed the Plains and planted grass,
I made the devil kiss my ass.

I don't know what the house made of the home that surrounded them. Every night I listened for their praise, hiding behind the window onto the dining room with my ear turned to catch the flickers of their conversation.

. . . name was, said Anne.

Rocket, borrowed her shoes, said Marian.

window? said Anne.

After seven . . . Holiday replied.

As the weather warmed they began to leave the windows open, and I know the sweet air charmed them; so I waited for a song back from the girls, though I wasn't sure what I was listening for. I knew if it were my house I would have hired an orchestra to sit in the windows and play music until midnight; but it wasn't my house, I was just a guest, and it was a strange house to me, with its lovely women and their fine manners, the walks they'd learned in dancing school (every Wednesday afternoon, in a smelly and haunted brick hall next to the hardware store downtown), the small, tasteful jewelry, seemingly painted on with a very fine brush (Olivia wore an antique silver and amethyst ring on her right hand, interchangeable earrings, and a tiny silver chain around her neck; Marian wore a single pair of silver earrings, and Anne wore gold), the rituals of borrowing and advising, and the fact, so curious and impressive to me at the time, that they were never bored.

In time they became giddy. The girls would collapse into fits of giggles at no point at all, laughing together until they snorted when they tried to talk. One night they decided together that they weren't going to speak for the rest of the night; instead they'd sing, and soon even the most banal comments were couched in melodies. The next day they chose to switch names: Olivia, lend me your grey cardigan, Olivia said to Marian. Sure, Marian, said the older to the younger, and they both went into her bedroom, emerging noisily a few minutes later: Olivia had a half dozen of her sister's sweaters and was wearing them all. She banged into the door frame and rebounded like a pinball, and Marian laughed so suddenly that she spit.

Later that week, while their parents were out to dinner, Marian worked up a dance to a song on a record she'd bought and showed it to Olivia. Come here, come here, come here, she said. Look at this. I call it the Ass Dance.

Half-squatting on the floor, she waggled and swayed, and swiveled and humped, in circles around the kitchen table while the song played loudly in the next room. She stopped and balanced with her hands on the linoleum, then thrust her rear end into the air, so that her hair fell in her reddened face and her shirt fell down her front. Then she turned a short somersault, barely missing a trash can that was sitting on the floor at the end of the countertop, and ended up in a squat again. She got up to a crouch, turned, pumped her arms like a chicken trying to fly, held her hands out on her extended arms like an Indian dancer—and fell into the table, knocking over an empty glass, which started rolling towards the edge: Olivia lunged at it, lost her balance and fell, bringing the whole thing halfway down with a huge crash. It missed her sister by just a few inches, though a piece of wooden chair that had been shattered underneath did fly off and hit her arm. There was silence.

God, are you all right? said Olivia. I'm so sorry.

Marian was lying against the refrigerator. Oh, shit, she said, and laughed: they both laughed, and then Marian slapped the floor with the palms of her hands. Come on, Olive Oyl, let's go for a walk. We can clean this up later.

All right, but don't call me Olive Oyl.

Why not, Olive Oyl?

If you do I'll call you Marvin.

I don't care. Come on, Olive Oyl. She got up from her chair and started out the door. Coming, Marvin.

Marian threw her shoulders back, took her sister by the arm, and started to march out of the room. We're the Miller sisters, she said. Marvin and Olive Oyl. Don't fuck with us—and at that moment the door shut behind them, and I didn't see them again until the next day, when they left the house together on their way into town.

If the girls were dizzy on sweet champagne, Anne warmed like a snifter of brandy in a taster's hands. She sang old songs as she went about the house. She switched to a brighter shade of lipstick. Her walk slowed and settled farther into her hips. One afternoon when the girls were out of earshot—Marian was out, and Olivia was playing *Jelly Roll* on the piano—I heard her make a lewd, affectionate suggestion to Holiday, who in return only furrowed his brow and frowned.

My house was gone: his house was mine. While they slept I reordered the books on bookshelves by color, by city of publication, to make long, absurd associations among their titles; one night I gently moved a bird's nest I'd found in a magnolia tree at the edge of their property to a spot under the eaves by Olivia's room, so that the singing would entertain her. I put mint leaves in their coffee grinds and used lemon peels to sweeten the cistern. At midnight I relit the house, divided it into pockets of shadows by changing bulbs and bending lampnecks, until the places where they read and relaxed were moved to where I could best cover them, and I could hide where I wanted, and love and know.

Holiday and Anne began to bicker like a cartoon couple. I half expected to find her in the kitchen doorway brandishing a rolling pin; I thought he might come down one night in flannel pajamas and a knitted nightcap to sleep on the couch. She teased him about his overeating again, and anyway how was she supposed to get dinner on the table if he ransacked the refrigerator every night. He couldn't find his favorite suit, the one he'd bought in New York, and he was annoyed by the way she laughed at his absentminded-ness. And she was spending too much money, he didn't know how, and then she bounced a check that she couldn't even remember writing. There were twigs and leaves all over the living room floor: couldn't they keep the house clean? She didn't care. I heard her purring to herself as she pruned an overgrown houseplant for the third time in a week, her cheeks flushed, her eyes heavy-lidded.

That Saturday Holiday woke up early, dressed, and set off for work, only to find his office closed. When he came home again he blamed his wife for not stopping him, although she'd been fast asleep when he left. That Sunday at midnight I planted belladonna among the flowers, whispering all the while:

Sing oh! for a goblin's life
Sing oh! for the life that's best
Sing oh! for a goblin's wife
And to hell with all the rest.

You will scoff at how haphazard I was, as if I were some home-grown Hamlet. His O was naught compared to mine. You'll think me irresolute and dull, and you'll dismiss me. I don't care. Every night as I returned to my bed I called the garden in, called it closer. It did come. In time the house almost disappeared into the foliage; they had trouble getting through the vines that hung down over the doors. Low clusters of grapes hung over the back patio; they jostled one another as they grew, until they shook free and dropped from their own weight, spattering the flagstones with blue juice. The rooms inside were as steamy as a hothouse, the air was charged with oxygen, and the houseplants grew strong and fertile, as if modeling the strength of the garden outside. Holiday's mansion became a luxury liner lost at sea, and I became the sea.

9

I was everywhere in that house, an extra, unforeseen member of the family. I listened in on each conversation, spied on each sleep. It became my avocation: if Olivia yawned, I saw. If she sat down and then stood up again, I saw. If Anne took longer in the bathroom in the morning, evaluating herself with her hands, if her husband dialed a wrong number, if he changed his shirt before dinner, if he muttered a name in his sleep, I knew. No gesture was made without me, no midnight snack silently stolen from the refrigerator that my watchful eyes didn't mark. I knew where the living room floorboards squeaked, knew the angles from the attic windows.

It had been a while since the girls even bothered to say good-bye when they left the house, but Holiday began to stop them as they rushed towards the door, and he'd ask them where they were going, and with whom, and for how long; and if he wasn't happy he'd keep them in. At the start Marian did as she was told; I remember, in particular, an overnight birthday party that she missed because Holiday blocked the door. But after a week or two had passed she began to ask him Why? with an expression of dismay and offense. Then she started to argue with him, and once she simply waited until he and Anne had gone out to dinner, then left the house on foot, headed for a midnight picnic under the river bluff. When he came home and discovered her gone he decided to wait up for her, but she didn't return until early the next morning and by then he'd fallen asleep on the couch in the living room. When he awoke it was almost dawn and she was already in bed.

Apparently he went to her room and woke her, and there was some kind of terrible fight. I was in bed myself by then, fast asleep in the boiler room, and I didn't see it, but Olivia remembered waking up to her father's yelling and finding the lights on in the hallway, and pale-faced, dark-eyed Marian standing in her doorway in her underwear, staring defiantly at Holiday as he ranted. Anne tried to make light of it the next evening as she and Holiday were getting ready for bed, but he was still angry. Can't have this, he muttered.

Oh, leave the girl alone, she said, and touched her husband gently on his chest. She's just having some fun. But Holiday's dark stares at his eldest daughter continued for a week.

Olivia was more retiring than her sister, and as Holiday became more of a captor she became almost reclusive. Instead of going out at night she would go upstairs to read, or into the music room to practice the piano. Nonetheless, he began to watch her carefully, as if he were afraid she was planning to leave him forever, and then in anger at his own fear he became hard on her. He snapped at her when, in her sweet, thoughtless way, she forgot to close a window before a rainstorm, or knocked the dishes together while she was clearing the dinner table. He watched her from head to toe as she crossed a room, as if her very body were something she'd failed to get right—breasts on a girl like you? and where'd you get those hips?—until she became so self-conscious that she stumbled and blushed; he refused to kiss her goodnight anymore. Aren't you a little bit old for that? he said.

She served the sentence quietly and without quite understanding, but she didn't let it disturb her powerful peace. I mean she was sugar.

10

Like sugar she began to melt and burn. She became sick with a sticky fever; it was with her when she woke up, opening her eyes amidst the smell of mud and sweet green garden fuses that had drifted under the window and into her room one warm spring morning. The girl hardly had enough energy to get out of bed. I watched from a crack in the basement door frame as she sat at the kitchen table, a plate of warm, gelatinous eggs before her. She stared at each forkful as if the food were ashes. Her face was pale.

Are you feeling okay? Marian asked, and her mother looked up and studied her, then leaned over and put the palm of her hand to Olivia's forehead. The girl shut her eyes and kept still. You're hot, Anne said. How do you feel?

Sick, Olivia answered. Tired. I'm not hungry.

Go back to bed. I'll call the school.

So Olivia went back up to her bedroom, pulled the shades, climbed under the covers, and slept for six more hours. The morning disappeared, and the afternoon was fading when she woke up again, went to the bathroom, and splashed water on her face. Her once clear eyes were cloudy with sleep, her nostrils pink around the edges. She was back in bed by nine that night.

When another day passed and Olivia wasn't better, Anne called the family doctor, who appeared solemnly at their door just before dinner and was led straight up to her room. He stayed there for a quarter of an hour; when he came out Anne was waiting in the hall, and I was waiting in the darkness at the top of the stairs to the attic. He shrugged and whispered.

It's probably just a bad case of flu, Anne said to Holiday in the living room. He said to wait a few days, and then call him again if it doesn't get better.

The next night Marian came home obviously drunk, her mouth slack, her walk uneven, and her clothes unkempt, covered with burrs and grass stains. She tried to slip past her father but she stumbled in the foyer and the noise alerted him. He came out of his study and stood in the door at the top of the stairs, waiting for her; when she raised her crazy eyes and saw him there she gave him a pained look and started to push past him; he took her forcefully by the arm. She tried to twist away; he squeezed and she yelped. You're going to wake your sister, he said, and then demanded loudly to know where she'd been. Swaying on her feet, staring at the ground for balance, she looked up at him slowly. I was out with some friends, she said, slurring her words a little.

No one wants you, he said suddenly, and then paused, embarrassed by the senselessness of his remark.

Marian looked up at him from under her brow, wearing an expression at once grievous and furious. A cumulus piled down into the hallway, thickening in an anvil shape above their heads. A mob ran past her into the rain—

Suck my dick, she said, then laughed a little and started to turn away; he tugged her back by her arm and hit at the side of her head with one open hand, slapping her awkwardly to the ground—suddenly she was lying on her side with her hand raised over her head to fend off another, her hair in her face, her hand to her cheek, hot tears falling through her helpless fingers. He stood above her, trembling.

Sobbing, with a shock that smothered her anger, she jerked her arm out of his grasp, and still on her hands and knees she pulled herself across the hall into her room, reached up for the handle, and pushed the door open. Before he could react she'd thrown herself inside, turned and twisted on her hip like a landed fish flopping on the floor of a boat, and slammed the door shut behind her.

A beat passed while Holiday stood in the hallway. Then he went to Marian's door, reached his knuckles up to rap, changed his mind, and let his hand drop again. Like the agents of a body's blood, the family began to move: Anne came to the threshold of their bedroom and watched silently as he turned and started downstairs. From

94

Marian's room came the sound of something shattering against the door (it was a porcelain lamp base, a gift from her grandmother, and she would regret breaking it forever). A moment later Olivia's door opened and the girl came out. She stopped for a moment to rub the sleepy bewilderment from her eyes and then crossed the hall to her sister's room, where she knocked, spoke a word or two, and then, as the door opened just far enough for her to fit, slipped quickly inside. End of act umpteen.

11

Lights up on a circus ring. Midstage: monster. Feats of daring follow. One night, for example, I wrote an enormous O in bluegrass on the front lawn, homage to my unknown muse, a shade darker than the spears the firm had planted. It could hardly be seen from the ground, or even from the first-floor windows, but from the attic it was unmistakable, and in fact Holiday found it one weekend afternoon when he was up there searching for a box of papers, and had it pulled up the next day, though it took at least a week for the now-brown ring to disappear entirely. As they sat over coffee one evening later that same week, I slipped out into the dusk and made a planting of some phosphorescent algae in the fish pond so that at night it would shine with a greenish yellow cast. I'd found the rare and fragile stuff in a pet store in town, and while the light it eventually gave off was not the ghostly, electric glow that I'd hoped for—and had expected from the crude cartoon on the cover of the small white sack in which it came—I thought it was an interesting touch anyway.

12

In the garden, in the garden haze, I saw Marian walking briskly, wearing an expression so determined that I followed her, trotting slightly behind her and off to one side. Baker was in the front yard, clearing the grass catcher of a lawn mower. A moment later he started it up again, and the sound of its motor rose over the house and settled lazily down in the garden heat. Spot was on his hands and knees, pruning plants in the tomato patch, and as soon as Marian was within shouting distance she called to him without breaking her stride. Hey! she said, and he turned his head up and gave her a questioning look. Me? he mouthed, and gestured to his chest with a mud-spattered trowel. She didn't answer. Instead she stopped a few feet away from him, reached dramatically into the pocket of her jacket, pulled out a magazine, and began to brandish it at him. As soon as he recognized it he flinched, briefly looked to his right, as if hoping there were something there to carry him away, and then lowered his eyes. Is this yours? she demanded.

Where did you get that? he said, his eyes on a patch of grass just to the right of her right leg.

Is it yours?

Finally he looked at her, his face flushed and his eyes wet. That was in the truck, he said, softly.

The truck is in my driveway, she said, and shook the pages at him. What are you doing bringing something like this to my house?

I don't—

How dare you bring this around here. It's disgusting. She planted her feet and held the magazine by one corner so that it fell open in the sunlight, and I could see, even from a distance, the pale figure of a bare young woman on her back, her legs bent up as if she were balancing a large, invisible beach ball on the soles of her pink feet. There were two men bent over her. I had a sudden, absurd flush of worry for all three of them, buck naked and vulnerable as they were amid the branches and brambles of the garden.

Spot looked away. I thought if he got any redder he would burst like a piece of fruit, spattering the ground with seeds and bits of pulp. It's only . . . he said. Look, I'm sorry.

Marian closed the magazine and put it in her pocket again and then looked him up and down while he stood motionless, afraid to move. If you ever . . . she said, and spun on her heel. While she walked back to the house he went hastily back to his digging, though by the time she was at the back door the stubborn blows he made against the ground were utterly, ridiculously ineffectual.

She disappeared into her room, taking the magazine with her. She was locked away for the rest of the day, and no sound came from behind her door. Only very much later did I learn that she had been flipping through the pictures and thinking about herself, about boys and their incalculable want. She was bothered by the odd, too-sweet smell of the paper on which the photographs were printed; every time she turned a page it would come again. Occasionally she would pause and examine a spread; there was a secret somewhere, she knew, but nothing, no pose, no crevice or slope, seemed to hold a place for excitement to hide. She stripped her clothes off and compared herself frankly in the mirror on her closet door, posing herself in the afternoon sun as she thought a girl might, watching herself as she thought a boy might. She touched herself and caught, very briefly, a glimpse of the rude popularity she was looking for: her heart raced for a second: it was as if she'd turned her sex inside out like a glove and then tried to fit it back on her hand. The sensation passed, leaving her with a little touch of dizziness and a flush in her cheeks. She came down that evening to have dinner with her parents, and the look on her face was of perfect perplexity.

There were three of them at the table those days; Olivia was still ill, not getting better, not getting worse. Each evening her mother would bring her a tray of food and leave it for her to pick at. Each night they'd tiptoe past her room, afraid she'd wake if a floorboard creaked. After her meal on that evening Marian returned to her room, only to emerge again a minute later with the magazine hidden beneath her shirt. She entered her sister's room and shut the door behind her, and for the next hour they sat together and talked, a conversation of which I heard only one short part, the younger girl's sudden, loud giggling as Marian showed her the pictures.

13

As a rule Olivia started her homework at eight, though as the spring grew later she would sometimes wait until the sun had gone down. When she was ready she'd call a friend from a phone that her mother had brought her and placed by her bed, and would diligently write down in her notebook the work that her teachers had assigned, the exercises on pages 67–70 of *Second Year Algebra*, say; a chapter on Reconstruction in her social studies text (*The American Experience*); a poem by Poe for her advanced English class, with relentless feminine rhymes and a singsong meter that troubled her every night for a week as she tried to get to sleep. When at last she turned to her French lesson she pronounced the words out loud, *je veux, tu veux, il veut, vous voulez, nous voulons, ils veulent*, but softly, murmuring the unfamiliar phrases as if they were temptations to powers that she wasn't sure she wanted.

If she had favorites among the subjects they were hidden inside her head: her concentration caused her to frown over everything. The effort took its toll on the end of the only instrument she ever wrote with, a red-barreled fountain pen with a golden nib; it sat between her teeth as she thought, and she alternately chewed and sucked it as the words appeared and then vanished again. Out it came, the reversed cap still glistening from the sweet wetness of her mouth as she held it poised over the page, then crossed out a clause; in it went again, tipping up to her nose as she pursed her lips. Her handwriting was a girlish, eccentric half-script scribbled at a generous slant, within which fat loops appeared like loose threads in a seam, as if her thoughts were slightly unsure stitches in soft, deeply textured cloth. Upon finishing each night she'd turn to her diary for a while, and then, just before bed, hand the school papers over to her sister and say, Please don't read this, okay? Marian would deliver them to her teachers the following day, at the same time picking up the corrected pages of the day before. Her marks, I should say, were always high, and remained so until the school year ended. It ended—her indulgent mother let the girl go in on the last day, to cheer the coming summer with her friends—just a few days before Olivia and I met for the second time.

14

There was no reason for the hour I chose, though I would have liked to have had one. It was a Tuesday, and it was time, that's all. That night I lay on my back in bed as late as I could last and listened to the house make its midnight noises, the sudden cracks of the beams, the irregular pops of a window frame cooling, the rustling of a window sash above an air duct. A bright green parrot appeared from nowhere and perched in my thoughts. It pecked rapidly, silently, repeatedly at a wooden orange in a wooden bowl and then flew off again, dropping a single emerald feather that melted like a candy in my heated thoughts, leaving behind a slight sweet lime taste. I tried to ignore myself; instead, I imagined the lost pages of my father's book, posted the bones, felt the hard muscles and followed the veins, gave them nerves and wrapped the skin around them, savoring each addition as if I still held the pictures in my hands. When I was done it was still quiet, and I knew I couldn't wait any longer. I got up, smoothed my shirt, and began to tiptoe up the stairs.

When I came to Olivia's door I stopped. As I stood there, not moving, my seventeen years compressed into a minute that inflated like a soap bubble, with its reflected colors swimming and distorting on its expanding edge, a delicate sphere that soon detached and began to float slowly upwards on a current of warm air—and then burst when I finally touched her doorknob.

I was tender with the door; I closed it carefully behind me and stood at the foot of her hot bed, and my head filled with her un-nameable scent, its specific gravity, the oil of her inflamed skin and her singular perfume. I was numb from the ache of sweet anticipation. There were strange electrons coursing through my nerves; my chest was a battery, heavy, warm and alive with artificial energy, and I thought the hum would wake her. It didn't: for a full five minutes

I stood motionless in the darkness and watched her sleep under the moonbeams, so still, so quiet, a form under the bedclothes, slowly breathing, dreaming . . . a dark desk, a picture frame on the wall, its midnight glass reflecting my own uneven silhouette, a single shoe on the rug, a shelf of books and delicate mementos . . . I moved to the edge of her bed, and then sat slowly on one side and watched her until she woke up from the weight on her mattress, and—

She sat up suddenly and stared. Hello? Out came a soft, bare hand; when it met my wrist she dropped it gently back on the blanket.

Hello, I said. Her hair was matted and damp, and the bedclothes formed a second skin over her flesh. How are you?

Mmmm, don't know, she said, while her plump hands traced idle circles on the covers. She looked down from my face to her own covered body, blinking as if to see if she was still there. I touched a pair of fingertips to the side of her leg, drawing her eyes to my hand. I could feel the heat of her delirium escape through the blanket. I was a mirage, a ghost shimmering in the headlights. Who are you? she asked, not alarmed, curious. Her eyes opened wide and then dropped half-closed again.

No one, I answered, and held up my threadbare arms as proof. Don't worry. I bent to kiss her cheek; she offered it casually, made a slight noise with her lips, smiled softly.

How did you get here? she asked.

I was made here.

No you weren't. How did you get here?

I live in the basement.

Why?

Back to sleep, I said.

No, she insisted. Talk to me; I can't sleep anymore.

Can't talk now, I said, and slipped away again.

15

You didn't think I'd hurt her, did you? Did you think I could? From out of my years as a ghost? The stars would have fallen from the sky, to die as glittering litter on their front lawn. I'd never before wanted anything and I'd never again want anything else, but I needed to be met in kind, or else the self that made my wanting possible would vanish like an afterimage at the edge of sight. I didn't know anything, I'd never known anything, and my desires were like a film out of focus: for all their force, still undescribed. I was out of time, out of place, like a pauper on stage at the ballet, his hat in his hands, his eyes wide. I'm saying, I didn't know about girls and their ways, I didn't know what was expected of me. I was counting on some atavism to prompt me. When it failed to show I went into the garden, built a nest out of scavenged scraps of self-scorn, placed an egg inside, and waited for something, anything, to break out.

16

Shhh. Holiday is by his daughter's bedside, his wide frame awkwardly hunched over in the girl-sized chair he's pulled over from her desk. It's late in the afternoon, but the shades are down over the windows and the room is dark and isolated. Not a word, not a footstep, not a sound.

How's my little girl? he asks. The family doctor was by this morning to take a few drops of her precious, sluggish blood. She hadn't flinched when the needle went in, but as soon as he was gone she peeled the bandage from the crook of her arm, and she spent most of the day with her forefinger absently resting over the tiny, blood-blue bump. Late this afternoon a tentative diagnosis of mononucleosis was phoned in to Anne. Plenty of rest, plenty of fluids, not to worry. She called Holiday at the office and he came home early, and now sits in her bedroom. We haven't spoken in a while, he says. You know I've been busy at work.

I know.

Your mother says you slept all afternoon.

I did, I'm sorry, she replies, and he, not even catching the absurdity of her apology, goes on to ask her—no, instruct her—to get well. She sighs and looks down at her hands.

Watch carefully, now: he is about to change everything. He hikes his cuffs up so he can cross his legs, leans forward in his seat, and frowns. Do you know, he asks his lonely daughter, his bored daughter, who sleeps too much and thinks too much and aches from both, who loves her sister, who believes that her father is to be admired, whom a boy like me wants the way a prisoner wants parole, Do you know why Marian is being so difficult? I know you know. You do. I want you to tell me if she's keeping something from me.

Olivia turned over in her bed and lay there silently until her father put his hands on his knees, sighed loudly, stood, and left the room.

17

That night while she slept I put a present on her dresser top, a large, clear marble with a blue glass coil suspended in it. The next night I stole in and left her a sprig of lilac I had grown, the night after a small blank book bound in dark green cloth, with a black ribbon to hold it shut. Each time I returned I noticed the previous item had been carefully worked into her room; the marble went into a cup on her shelves, the lilacs into a beveled crystal glass she'd stolen from beneath the sideboard in the living room, the book gone, presumably in a drawer. A small brass bell was next, then a new nib for her pen, then a map of the world. At last I left a small, impossibly ugly doll, a homunculus only a girl could love, with bulging eyes and wild hair, and a rubber belly, punctuated by the pock of its deep navel, that hung over its belt line—a troll, in fact, an effigy and a promise.

I waited to approach her again. I let her lie in bed, because I knew that even as I waited she was thinking; and with her thinking, she was changing. Had she heard her own voice back she might have wondered where those words had come from, but she'd never been angry before, and however long her temper had been in coming she was so unused to the sensation that she mistook it for a tension her sickness had described. To admit that her father had lost hold of her affections was like settling alone in a new town; but I knew and I was waiting to welcome her there. When the days had passed and she'd settled, I checked my trembling, came out of the basement, and headed straight up the stairs.

From the moment I crossed the threshold of her room I felt a kind of enchantment, as if I'd stepped into storybook chambers, outside of which was not a house but a child's bookshelf, so that upon opening the door again I'd find a raft of adventuring sailors on a dark blue sea, or a sultan's cave of shimmering riches. I locked the door from the inside so that we wouldn't be disturbed, and when I turned back I could see the shadows of her dresser, a faint grey image framed on the wall, her bed with its mysteries, her hillocks on the plains. There had been an electrical storm earlier in the night, and the air was thick with ozone. Olivia lay sound asleep with her blanket drawn up to her neck, her hands over her head, one set of fingers curled lightly around the post of the headboard, the other bent beside her ear.

I woke her by placing my left hand on her covered left hip until she stirred. She raised her head calmly, and her eyes were clear: Oh, hello again, she said, and sighed. A minute passed while the room filled with ancient, silent static, the noise of a phantom radio tuned to the spaces between the stars. You're the boy from our party, aren't you? she asked. I saw you in the garden last week. So sleepy. I nodded.

Did you leave me those things? I nodded again. That was sweet, she said, and then sighed: it sounded like the rustle a hand makes in a candy jar. My father's going to kill you.

He might, I said. How are you feeling? I brushed a strand of her hair from her cheek.

Okay, she said. She frowned. Who are you?

18

Exterior of the dark house. Sound of crickets.

19

I said, It's true I'm an incubus, a disturbance, a ripple in your reverie. I said, Let me lie here and watch, seeing over you while you sleep there, selfless and unashamed, your face unhidden, your body bare beneath your blanket. You've heard stories, and they are true, of how the monkey got a monkey's face, how turtles sleep inside their shells, how worms eat dirt and birds eat worms. And at night fish swim slowly through your room, sculling silently in your dreams: there's a flash of silver skin, there's a hand upon your arm . . . Here, draw back the bedclothes, I said. Put down the shades.

You do talk, she said. But I know who you are, and I knew this would happen. And then without the slightest warning she tipped her head back and drew a breath, arched under my hand and parted her trembling limbs, exposing her tender, pale belly. Then she reached up for my shoulder and, brooking no denial or disbelief, pulled me down to her.

20

A first kiss is an element of supernature; there's no preparing for the shock of the lips first opening, of the slick tongue licking, of the taste of being tasted. There's the life of the beloved, the effortless, ongoing bellows of her body, her quickening eyes, the graceful shift of her limbs, her gulps and gasps, in a subtle breath that enters through her humid mouth, and leaves with particles of spent appetite. I bent over Olivia, but I couldn't see her eyes, only her warm, smeary lips as they opened to expose her mouth, a dark flash of her tongue, her sweet, hot breath as she sighed, and kissed me. And then?

Puella. It's a long story.

Ring of Fire

1

When I awoke the following morning I was alone in her soft bed, with her yellow blanket pulled over my legs. There was sun under the window shades, and a bittersweet scent in the air. My skin was tender from the night before, my mouth still swollen and filled with an awkward taste. I could see my clothes in a small pile next to a pillow that had landed on the floor during the night, and her nightgown draped neatly over the back of the chair at her desk. Legs entangled in a shroud, a twisted sheet, I unraveled it and pressed it to my chest. It smelled slightly sour. The house was stalled, dead quiet, but I could hear a faint droning through the window from a tiny plane passing overhead, the dim white ceiling of her room, the sky.

I'd just resolved to sit up when the door opened and she came in, wearing a pair of navy blue sweatpants and a black, black-buttoned jersey. She crossed the floor and stopped at the foot of the bed, where she stood and watched me with a half-smile on her lips as I hastily pulled the bedclothes over my midriff. Down went her hand, and she grabbed the bottom of the blanket and pulled it away again, leaving me with only a sheet to cover myself, and still she watched me, still smiled.

Good morning, she said at last, in a voice like a country church bell. It's ten-thirty, you have to get up. It's a good thing I woke up early, or else my mother might have come in. She went to the window and jerked down on the shade, releasing it so that it flew up and flapped around the roll and a burst of sunlight leaped into the room. And I have to wash these sheets before she gets back. With that she reached down again, took hold of the top linen, and tore it off the bed, and as it hung to the floor from one hand she gestured towards a few sienna spots on the bottom sheet with the other. You see, she said. That's what happens. Now, come on.

She was all business for the next few minutes. She handed me my pants and turned away as I pulled them on, and she had the mattress stripped and was standing in the doorway before I'd buttoned my shirt. Everyone's gone out, she said matter-of-factly. I'll be back in a second, don't go anywhere.

But as soon as the door shut behind her I was gone: I ran to snowy Alaska, then sailed across the straits to Asia, wandered down through the steppes of Mongolia and crossed into vast, pale green China. There I hid in a farmhouse, drinking tea from a white porcelain bowl and passing pleasantries with the peasantry, until the door opened and glancing-eyed Olivia came in. She looked at the unmade bed, then at unmade me. She rubbed her nose with back of her hand, looked at the floor, looked at me, at the floor, out the window, at me. For a moment I thought that she'd forgotten everything, our numb introduction, the soft, sudden wrack of her body—and sleeping on her side afterwards, with her legs entwined with mine, her back against my chest and her backside pressed into my hips. Suddenly she laughed as if she had been tickled by a ghost and said, Marian . . . never mind. This is weird, it really is. I mean . . . you won't tell anyone, will you?

Me? I thought. I don't know anyone, here's to ten thousand miles of highway. No, I assured her out loud. She examined my face and then lowered her lashes. Okay, she said. Well look, Wilson . . . I think you'd better go now.

At once I stood and started blindly into the hall, and she followed me out as far as the threshold of her room. When am I going to see you again? She asked as I reached the stairs.

Again is such a pretty word, a joining arc in a comforting circle of time. I turned around. Tonight, if you'd like, I said.

Come here. Taking me by both hands she stood up on her toes, quickly kissed my cheek, put her lips to my ear, and whispered. Then she backed through her door until our arms were outstretched like suspension cables on a bridge, slowly slid her damp fingers away, smiled briefly, and turned into her room. When she shut the door I was left alone in the hallway, with the heat from her hand melting on mine.

Exit, pursued by a bear.

2

Her mind remained febrile through the following days, but I was there to distract her: I went to her every night, early if her parents were out at dinner or visiting friends, late if I had to. She would always be awake and waiting for me when I arrived, and she would always be relieved that I'd made it to her safely, always a little bit puzzled by my ability to move through the house without being felt, always excited that at last she had a secret worth keeping. They were a polite family, they knocked before coming into her room, and Olivia would ask them to wait a second. I was a character she had invented, a young boy dreamed by a young girl who was confined to her bedroom in her parents' house for too long, a lover she had conjured up to help her pass the hours.

The hours passed. I felt a wild English in my soul, and any moment that I couldn't be with her I grew dizzy with impatience and curiosity. While she was awake I entertained her with tales of my troubles and adventures, and she listened to them all with perfect peace, and told me her own as if they had been written in anticipation of my coming. When I sang her to sleep:

> The lights go down, the music ends
> Say goodnight to all your friends
> Take my hand, and we'll get lost
> To the tune of the Mississippi Waltz

she slept, for an hour, or an afternoon, or a week.

From here the time we had together looks like no time at all; however distended it may have been it had no duration, and nothing moved. We would not fall away. We were perpetual children in perpetual motion, and she smiled and smiled; I stole kisses from her now and then just to make sure she wouldn't mind, tentatively held the undercurve of her breast, bussed her shoulder while she smiled curiously. I danced like an ape at the foot of her bed, I was Olivia's fool,

I could say anything, so long as it was either right, or wrong enough to make her laugh. Except—the first time I told her of my natural state, of my goblinhood, she frowned and dismissed the fact with one graceful wave of her pale hand. The second time she laughed uncomfortably. When I told her again she grew angry with me and told me harshly not to say anything about it again. So I put that letter down—anyway it was dying—shifted my weight, and lay my head in her lap so I could listen to her stories.

They wandered like an unfortunate sailor on the dips and swirls of her voice, its changing currents, the effort when it rose on a rock, the sounds on which her tongue caught and snarled like seaweed on a fishhook, weighing down the word. I memorized the manner of every note, how she burst words in exclamation, how she curled her mouth around a soft consonant, blotted one, ticked her tongue against another; some she allowed to drift into a smile; others she simply spoke with a wit that proved itself by hiding. You see, a woman and her body meet at a membrane, a thin, expressive film between her thoughts and the specific music her public knows: it is her voice. To this day I'd recognize Olivia's at the first word, the first vowel that her tongue produced, because I immediately loved her and loved to hear her.

It wasn't just her voice: I collected her habits as if they were coins: she was afraid of heights; she would blush with embarrassment at the way her tongue slipped out of her mouth when she laughed, then laugh at her embarrassment, grow embarrassed at that laughter, and dissolve into ingrown red-faced giggles; she would wriggle in response to the tip of my finger between two particular folds of skin . . .

I wondered at her body, how she softened into traces of fat where her ribs collapsed, leaving gummy sections above her hipbones, mounted on her cambered spine and the hard, narrow muscles of her lower back. I buried my blind mouth in the salty pit of her throat, the coarse patch on the back of her elbows, the thin line of sweat collected in the crease behind her knees, the private lining of her thighs, the sudden, stiff black hairs and slick, darkened crevices, warm puddles and ponds. How damp she was, how soaked with perspiration and saliva, hot tears in her eyes, balance water in her inner ear, and just beneath soggy skin a flush of blood and bile, sticky humors, sap, waste, lust and wetness. Kisses, kisses. I couldn't touch her body anywhere without raising a heavy, scented drop of molasses to my fingertip, or causing some part of it to move, a limb to shift, her belly to tighten, the tone or scent of her breath to change; I was fascinated by the resilience of the cups and bowls of flesh that enveloped the tubules and crimson gullies below, the numberless threads that attached them to her thin spine and rigged splinters of bone; I could mold the porous surface with my hands, and still each damp part would return to its place, albeit reddened by a blush of blood that had risen to the spot where the surface had been abraded, and which was all there was to mark her with the suggestion that she hadn't been alone, a fleeting sign of the contingency, the particularity of our engagement.

When I was inside her I could feel the strength she drew on to hold me, never leaving me, never faltering. I would give myself up and brace myself to fall into her, hugely, half-terrified, out into nothing, her powerful O. I didn't know, I always ended in her arms, there was that familiar scent, familiar flesh against my cheek; she was still there, beating beneath her breastbone, her hand on the base of my neck. I would nearly weep for sweet weakness and want of self.

I will now fold and seal this envelope, with its crumpled note and humid perfume, and carefully hide it away.

3

It was a clear Sunday afternoon, with a sky bluer than blue, and the air warm and just slightly damp. Holiday, Anne, and Marian were out on the back porch along with one of Anne's friends, a red-haired woman, in a blue dress who seemed to want to be elsewhere. I was in the attic, watching from the window. I wanted to hear them, so I pushed the glass up, raised the screen, and stuck my head out, but I was too far above them for the sounds of their conversation to reach me, and the angle from which I watched obscured their faces: I could read the motions of their bodies, but not enough to tell what kind of time they were keeping. Anne was brushing back a thin tree branch that had recently grown over the table, but each time she absently pushed it aside it would glide back before her face. Holiday was gesturing with one hand, and as he went on their guest leaned farther and farther back in her chair, like a timid swimmer trying to escape a giant wave. I could see her hands rise to her midriff in preparation for the blow.

It was not Holiday to whom she was responding: it was Marian, and he went on obliviously. Anne put her hand on her husband's for a moment, but he shook it off in the course of gesturing at his daughter, and then at the house. All at once Marian started to move; first she leaned forward, then she leaned back again, and I heard her voice as it rose to a hoarse shout. What's wrong with me! she yelled as she abruptly stood up from the table, spilling drinks into quickening laps. On her way into the house she halted and turned her head up towards me, squinting into the bright sky, and then dropped her eyes again and ran quickly into the house as I pulled my head into the attic and swore myself up and down for being careless.

4

Here, I have something for you.

For me?

You've been so nice about me being sick and all. It's just this little thing.

What is it?

It's just something I got. Open it. I'm not going to tell you.

She handed me a dark blue book-sized box. When I lifted the lid I found white tissue paper inside, folded over to cover the contents. With thumb and forefinger I delicately peeled back the translucent covers; beneath I discovered a dozen brown bulbs nestled together on a thin bed of white cotton. They were about the size of golf balls, and some had pale white tubules already poking through the surface. They gave off a faint odor of soil. I plucked one out and held it in the palm of my hand; it was as hard as a walnut from the compression of its patient cells. They're called orchid irises, Olivia said. The man in the store said they'd come up purple in the spring. I know you've been spending so much time with me that you haven't been able to work, so I wanted to give you something. If we plant them now, we can wait for them to come up. She nodded as she spoke, as if neither the words themselves nor her tone of voice, at once enthusiastic and questioning, were enough to convey her desire that we plant together, wait together, and then note what we had grown, and her confidence in the long association to which it testified. I replaced the bulb in the box, put the box on her night table, and then lay her down on her back on the freshly made bed, where I gave her a kiss as long as the Champs-Élysées.

My favorite thing from a book, ever, said Olivia as we were getting into bed later that evening, is that little man jumping up and down all by himself somewhere, when he thinks no one's looking, and singing, What a good thing it is, that no one knows, my name is Rumpelstiltskin.

5

The bulbs went into a secret corner of the garden later that night, away from the rest of the plants in a spot where I hoped they would form a secret patch of purple, unadmired by anyone but Olivia and me. Through the following days I tried to doctor the girl with attention, with a laugh late at night and a glass of water to wet her throat, with the drops of sweet love that I'd distilled over the day. In return she gave me a book, a kind of encyclopedia of occult arts and sciences, of which there existed only a single hand-written copy, bound in ocean blue. Together we leafed through its pages, randomly opening to one or another entry. In a chapter on botany we discovered a flower with large, fleshy petals that trembled and sweated at the merest hint of a stranger's approach. Under Sport we found a game for an unopposed team, to be played on a field abandoned after a summer rainstorm, when pond-like mud puddles appeared amid tufts of grass. Another entry described a kind of phenomenal origami for two, an art of topographic folds that made a stiffened nipple appear beside the rounded, covered plate of a kneecap, or the hanging drop of an earlobe press against an inner thigh. There were illustrations, too, of silver coins with tails on both sides, of the shy mouth of an upended bottle, of a fat lioness licking her belly lazily, or a fucked girl sighing thickly. Of other, less illuminated passages I'll remain silent, except to say that she was a very curious, very adventurous girl, a girl given to fits of surprisingly coarse appetite, a beautiful, greedy girl; that she laughed a lot and winced a few times; and that as her store of achievements grew she began to shine like a mirror at which someone has aimed a lamp.

6

Aside from the planting I just mentioned the house and its garden were left alone, and although her senses were often stopped and I had only the sound of her sea-slow breathing for company, I left our hideout only when I had to, saving my foraging in the refrigerator for the latest possible hours. I sang:

I got a girl, sweet sixteen
Damnedest thing I've ever seen
Sleeps all night, sleeps all day
And what she dreams I couldn't say.

Well I got a girl, she treats me nice
She loves me once and then she loves me twice
And when again she falls asleep
I give myself her soul to keep.

I remember taking her arm in my hand and gazing at it, admiring its composition, the pallor produced by so many layers of fine

116

translucence. I could see blue veins raised beneath, as if her blood had been replaced with warm saltwater. But I worried about what inner disability could have been rewritten into such outward beauty, so I used to try to wash away her sickness by opening the window to let in the cool, clear air, and then joining her in her hot bed again, where I would stroke her gently while she slept, as if to draw the illness out of her. I think of those first dreamy drops of morning, the fine grey cast out her window, Olivia waking within the compass of my unending and patient eye. I would forget the pointless movement of the clock, in those hours I spent patiently waiting for her to escape her oblivion, while the whole world, round as it was and surrounded by water, reveled in its roundness and gently revolved. So you can keep your money, and take my name, too; you can seat yourself at world's end and legislate like Solomon. I was seventeen, and knew neither the poet's lyric nor the schoolyard boast. She was sixteen and sick. But as long as I had Olivia I wouldn't have changed my lot with kings.

One night I came back from my dinner and found her in the bathroom, bending naked over the sink while she washed her face. She rose when I came in and smiled slightly at my reflection. I came up behind her and wrapped her in my arms. Her broad, naked hips hid mine, and her shoulderblades, still slightly clammy from her shower, pressed against my chest. Under the light I could see the inch-long scar on the front of her knee, the trace of an operation she'd had after falling from a horse a few years earlier (there was another, fishhook-shaped white line behind her ear, where her sister had hit her with a toy boat when they were children). She reached for a navy blue hand towel that sat amid the mess of her bath things on the counter before us, the English soap, an uncapped toothpaste tube with a blot of neon blue left extruding from the little nozzle at the end, a bottle of clear astringent, a red aerosol antiperspirant can. When she'd finished drying her face she looked up; I found my own image in the mirror, with hers before me, her head tilted slightly back to rest upon my shoulder, her spine curved until her shoulderblades pressed into my chest, her dark sweat-flattened curls framing her pale face. I put one arm around her waist, and with the other hand I gently cupped the dry

117

closure towards which her hips tended. The light above the bathroom sink was on and it raked down across us; her skin was dull and pale from her illness, and the surface just beneath her eyes was drawn and damp, as if from lust. As I watched her face her gaze moved gently back and forth between us, so that sometimes I caught her looking at herself, and sometimes her indolent eyes met mine. Strangest of all was when, sensing her watching me as I watched myself, I felt brief jolts of belovedness. Then I could see myself, not a beast but loved, and with an uncommon, terrible, almost unbearable generosity. When she finally pulled away to fetch a towel my hand was damp with a spoonful of slick, mossy attar.

7

Here is a photograph of the two sisters as little girls. It was in a silver frame on Anne's bedroom dresser, a well-worn charm stamped with a trellis of serrated leaves, a precious and permanent border between the scene inside and the violence of passing days. Now it is in my memory.

I asked Olivia about it once. She frowned as if she were annoyed that I'd settle on such a thing, when there was so much that was more important to know. It was an heirloom, she said, passed on from her great-grandmother to her mother some years past. You get it next, I said.

I suppose, she replied, and shrugged. Unless Marian does.

In the picture the two girls are sitting side by side on a short flight of marble stairs, while behind them looms the old oak door of a church, with a great brass ring doorknob and thick black hinges. Marian is about five, my Olivia perhaps three, and seems not so much a younger version of the girl I knew as a counterpart in some half-fictive metaphysical dimension. It's the afternoon of a cousin's wedding, and the two of them are flower girls; they're wearing white dresses trimmed with delicate lace and holding beribboned bouquets, and Marian has a small, crowning ring of white flowers in her hair. There are high-noon shadows on the stairs by their legs. Olivia is leaning so far over that she's sprawled onto her sister's lap, although she doesn't seem to notice; she's gazing obliquely down at something just beside Marian's shiny black shoes, her baby face wearing an expression of seriousness that borders on a pout. In contrast to her sweet absorption her sister seems positively theatrical: she looks out at the camera with a wide, gap-toothed grin, her elbows planted firmly on her knees, her small hands crossed under her sharp chin.

8

On the evening of the Fourth of July I went to visit my more majuscule O after dinner. The sun was just setting, and as the edge of the earth rose the clouds on the horizon turned into a red lipstick smear. It was going to be a hot night, the kind of night that cheated insidiously against screen doors and open windows, that made fat, bloody-wet babies born in April. Meet me by the pond in the backyard in twenty minutes, she said, and when I asked her why she put her hand to my mouth and then, as a joke, tucked the tip of one finger in upon my tongue. Just meet me.

I watched her as she sneaked out the back door and made her way across the lawn. She was wearing black jeans, a grey sweatshirt, and a pair of tan hiking shoes, and when she spotted me she hurried over, grabbed my hand, and pulled me across the grass towards the fence. Come on, she said breathlessly. If they know I'm gone . . . . When we reached the fence she stopped for a second, and then climbed it awkwardly, casting her leg up to the highest strand and throwing herself half over until, with her hair down, laughing, she fell onto her feet on the other side. Come on, she said. I vaulted over to her side. Olivia, I said. Oh, shut up, she answered, and stuck her thick tongue out at me. Then she grabbed me by the hand again and led me running across the street and up the dark driveway of the neighbors behind. Shhhh! she said loudly. We skirted the side of the house and then crossed into the next yard. Watch out, she said as we came upon a patio with a swimming pool sunk in it, the moon dissolving into an ivory slick on its surface.

I was lost, running to keep up with her as the shadowy yards and fences passed, another road, a small copse of town trees, a road again, and then a chain link fence that she fell against breathlessly, causing the metal to rattle softly and distend inward. Behind it was a closely planted wood, so dense that it was impossible to see more than a few yards into the trees. She put one foot through a diamond in the fence, turned to me, and said, Help me, will you? Overhead a tower of high tension power lines buzzed softly. I could feel her feverish skin through her shirt as I steadied her.

The woods proved to be an illusion; a few quick blind steps brought us to the edge of a golf course, a fantastic landscape at that hour with its rolling, close-cropped fields and far tiers of trees, among which the blue dusk collected in darker, gauze-grey patches. Now, you've got to keep down, she said before she took off again. I followed in a crouch across a wide felt lawn, around a large pond, across another strip of grass, and then to the edge of a sand pit, which took both of us so completely by surprise that together we tumbled down into its soft, firm drifts. She let out a laugh and immediately began crawling clumsily back up towards the top, with me in pursuit. Look, she said as we arranged ourselves, side by side, with our heads just over the lip. Over there. She pointed to a building about a quarter of a mile away over the grass. I could see a line of cars parked in front of it, and a ragged line of dark figures gathered up to the edge of the green. This is where—

Oh! the sky blew open and an orb of red sparks rapidly expanded above us. Olivia ducked as another, green ball went off with a bang. I think we're—white flash—I thought! she yelled as a series of rockets swirled in a cloud of grey smoke that had collected in the illumination. I was afraid that if I reached my arm up I would lose it at the elbow. Oh my god. It began to rain bits of hot metal, and she rolled over to brush firelets out of her hair as a bright cobalt burst snapped open in the sky directly overhead, and then another. The noise grew, and she threw herself against me; I lost my balance and we fell, rolling in a rough tangle down the soft slope to the bottom of the sand trap again. There was a green shadow on her face, and a crackling sound in the sky. She grabbed my arm and pointed; above us there was nothing but the vault of the heavens outlined by the edge of the pit, and dying sapphire embers: then two more explosions, red rockets and sizzling white stars that intermingled with one another and the shadows of the dead sparks as they landed in the sand beside us—another blue, unrelenting blue and emerald set of splashes, so low that they formed a triumphal ceiling over the pit, a dome of dumbstruck glory—and all at once the light grew and the percussion came faster and louder, lighting the air with fat flashes of white, and dense, symmetrical constellations suddenly expanding into soft motes and filaments of colored dashes. My ears began to ring painfully, my heart pounded in my chest, and my nostrils stung with the sharp smell of cordite. Olivia let out a squeal and rolled on top of me, shaking and clutching my shoulders with her soft hands. Then she began whispering hotly in my ear, frantically relating some long point that I couldn't quite hear; before she'd gotten the first word out a barrage of cannon shots and copper fire began that I thought would ignite the air. I could feel her stomach pressed against mine, her hips between my hands as if I were taking her down from a tree, her crotch pushing excitedly against mine as she spoke.

And then it was over, just as the last words—*rest of my life*—slipped from her mouth. Applause drifted from across the lawn, and then car horns. I asked her to tell me what she'd said, but she frowned at me and then scrambled up the side of the sand, and when I followed her I found her crouched down on the edge of the grass. Together we watched the headlights flash; and then the spectators congratulated each other, climbed slowly into their cars, and drove away. Olivia stood and dusted the granules of sand from her thighs. Oh, she said. I'm so sorry, and she laughed. Get up. I didn't know it'd be right here. I really thought we were going to die. Get up. She came to me, took my hand, and tugged me until I got to my feet. I could feel her pulse beating through the moist skin on her wrist, and I bent forward to kiss her. No, she said, and instead wrapped her arms around me, lay her head on my shoulder, and squeezed me as tightly as she could. That night I heard her laughing in her sleep.

9

The heat at which the spring had hinted became full midway through the summer. Hardly a day went by in late July without a sunstorm interrupting the hours and enforcing an idleness that soon began to connect the month together, giving it a tone which a given afternoon might have lacked, but which, in retrospect, seems more real than any of our actions. I remember, for example, the idea of evenings that the day seemed to have exhaled more than I do any particular after-dinner stroll, and a blood-orange moon that sat motionless above the treetops for a week.

After everyone had gone to bed, I used to come down from Olivia's room or up from the basement and slip quietly through the dark house to the kitchen, where I would retrieve the day's newspaper from a pile of discards by the back door. One midnight I read that the captain of a barge on the river had fallen asleep at the helm the night before and had collided in the darkness with a motorboat. The latter sank, and the barge had cracked open so that its cargo—a shipment of sorghum, I think it was—spilled into the water.

Another night a windstorm tore off a large branch of a cherry tree in the front yard. It fell across the driveway, and Holiday had to wait the next morning until the gardeners arrived—forty-five minutes late. By cutting the limb into pieces with a loud chainsaw they managed to get him on the road by noon. When they were finished there were pale yellow drifts of sawdust on the blacktop.

A water pipe that ran behind the property burst one night later in the month, and the next morning the bottom half of the garden had become a silver reflection of the pale blue sky. Baker, Spot, and Willie were sent home.

Olivia sat in her room that afternoon, her skin dry and goose-pimply from her air-conditioning, and wrote a letter to her best friend, a classmate who'd moved off to Houston two years back. I snuck up to her as she was finishing it, and she folded it carefully in thirds and began to address an envelope as she described the girl to me. Her name was Susan, her mother was Mexican, her body was boyish, and her mind was wicked. She never left the house without taking along a camera and looking for a war.

—What do you want to be, anyway? she asked suddenly. The question was so unexpected that the first thought that came to me was, A rattlesnake. I said as much, and she opened her mouth in surprise and then laughed. No, be serious, she said.

Be serious? A vein of iron ore, a bass guitar.

Stop it . . .

A bucket of paint, a monkey's uncle, a pumpkin pie.

Shhh.

Why, what do you want to be? But by then she was mad at me and wouldn't answer; and the more I begged the more adamantly silent she was, until finally she said, Leave me alone! The batteries of the afternoon whirred down and went dead.

I raised the question again a week or so later, but instead of answering she stared at me as if I'd torn her clothing; I shrank, and she said, sarcastically, A potato bug. I never asked her again, so whatever distant occupation she'd imagined for herself—toy-maker? cardsharp? author?—was lost to me forever, evaporated in the summer sun like a poolside puddle.

Housebound and bothered by the hot, damp weather, the family became helplessly reliant on one another, and I was almost always hiding. There were not enough rooms. Holiday in particular took the heat badly; if he'd thought he could stop it by sheer force of will he would have tried, but it's not in a man to shed coolness. His birthday fell at the end of the month; he would be fifty-eight. Anne and Marian had planned a dinner out, but that evening he came home, hung his coat in the hallway closet, and went to find Anne.

I'd rather we stayed in tonight, he said. She was in their bathroom, putting on perfume. It's been a very long and tiring day. I've already called the restaurant and canceled our reservations.

Anne gestured at her body to indicate the silk slip she was wearing, but he was already halfway out the door. She was left to blush slightly, sigh heavily, and change her clothes again.

So there was a short, hastily fixed dinner at home (Olivia attended), followed by a brief, dry ceremony of presents, and then he went for a drive alone, leaving his wife and daughters to clear the table, watch a movie on TV, and reassure one another that, after all, he'd had a good time.

10

The king is in his counting house, counting out his money. The queen and one princess watch television in the living room, its bright chatter echoing through the house; and—quiet—behind the door of her darkened bedroom the younger heir has a secret audience with the jester. He shows her delightful tricks, performs feats of magic (now you see it, now you don't!), impossible stunts for her hot laughter. In a moment of fast emotion she said she loved me, and my heart inflated with rare motion at the exclamation, so that I didn't answer. She smiled at my expression.

A little later we heard a knocking at the door, and the period breached was so private that at first I thought someone was standing over her, asking permission to open her up like a Russian doll, not knowing that I was in there. Within a moment I had slipped out and scrambled into her bathroom, where I crouched behind her shower curtain, shivering and listening as he entered the room. What on earth are you doing in here? he asked, and I thought I heard him sniff the air slightly. Um, exercises, said Olivia breathlessly. The doctor said I should.

In the middle of the night? said Holiday. You can hear it out in the hallway.

Sorry, Olivia replied. I couldn't sleep. I'll try to make less noise.

. . . Later, I lay supine on the bed, and she sat like an outlaw astride my hips, her warm slick holding me; she cocked her head back gently to move her hair off her shoulder. Hush. Olivia was always trying to quiet me. She made a face from some effort inside her. Can you feel that? she whispered.

What?

I'm squeezing. She squinted again and something moved. There. Did you feel that?

A little, like a little grip.

I should work on that. Squeeze you. She rose up on her haunches slightly, bent over and put her hand over my mouth, and I could taste the invisible salt and sandpaper of her fingertips.

Later, the river quickened as it narrowed.

And later, she sat up against the headboard and began to tell me about her mother's family, a summer spent in a house by the beach with a dissolute uncle whom everyone but her aunt adored—but just as she'd started to describe the boat they took out into the Gulf she trailed off, turned her eyes away and mumbled, I'll never know what everyone else knows. Her voice was so soft that I had to ask her to say it again. I'll never know. I'll always miss the glances, always stare stupidly at a joke that everyone else gets, and . . . everyone will always treat me like a child. Her eyes were glassy with tears. All these things happen, and I don't understand why, she said. I don't understand what everyone wants, I don't understand what I'm supposed to do, I don't understand, what, why do I . . .?

She was shaking. I touched my hand to the back of her neck, high up under her falling hair, drew an encouraging breath, and began. Olivia, I said. Look at me: all I know is you. No one ever says anything. Come with me. Your grandmother, your mother had a father, but they left home. Your sister will go someday, and they'll be glad for her. You're no different; soon it'll be time for you, too. Please, you'll always be loved. Come with me.

She thought for a moment, with her head bowed until her chin rested on her chest and her hair fell over her face. I held my breath, held my hands still at my sides, held a blue-white pearl under my tongue. Her eyes slowly closed. Maybe, she said at last. Maybe.

11

She spent the next day in her bathrobe, reading in a chair in the living room. It was the second week in August, and even with the air-conditioning the heat seeped through the walls, and melted every bond. As the hours passed her pinned up hair came loose, until a long, curled lock reached the corner of her mouth, where she could blandly suck on it. By the time her mother came in from the kitchen with a glass of iced tea I'd darted off the patio and onto the grounds.

I was haunting a copse of trees just above the gazebo, and I decided to pay a visit to the place for the first time since I'd been cast out of it. It was like visiting a childhood home, ten years gone: once I had thought the Millers were on the far side of some impenetrable direction, like one's own back in a mirror, and I wanted to recapture that disproven perspective, so I started to cross the grass—but I heard a voice, and I had to turn back and crouch down beside the trunk. There, standing under the pitched roof, was the trio of workers, Baker, Spot, and Willie, leaning lazily against the balustrade.

They'd apparently been talking for a few minutes before I arrived; Baker's cigarette was burned down to the filter. They may have been planning for weeks before, but more likely it had occurred to them that morning. There's a window open into the basement, Spot was saying—he was referring to my way in and out. There's stairs up into the kitchen. All, the television, stereo and all are on the first floor.

Where are the bedrooms? Baker asked.

The parents sleep above the dining room, and the girls are above the kitchen. (Here pie-faced Willie giggled grotesquely and adjusted the fold in the front of his sagging pants.) But there are carpets on the floors. Besides, one girl is always sleeping, and the other one is never home. The old man has a study on the first floor, too, but he's usually in bed by eleven. So if we wait until, say, after one, we'll be okay . . .

Baker threw his cigarette butt out onto the lawn and spit after it. Wednesday?

Wednesday it was.

12

God is good and I'm a joker, a trickster, a comedian, a cartoon. Buster Keaton is my muse; I live in a slapstick world, with its happy props, its rubber masks, its breakaway bottles and bruised knees; I have a comic's love of sets and messes, and time and preposterous logic are my media. I waited for my foils on the night they'd named, made up with Olivia's gunk, my face slathered with fat dollops of her lipstick and mascara (she never used them: she said she'd bought them years ago). On my head I wore a bright red fright wig that I'd found in a charity store in town over the weekend. It was an overcast, inky black night, and at the crest of midnight I kissed my girlfriend on her cool, smooth forehead, went downstairs to the basement, and waited with my trouble in mind.

A calm, contemplative hour passed. I thought of Olivia, asleep upstairs, and began to whisper this song:

If it's yellow, then it's clear,
If it's clear, then there's sun,
If there's sun, then there's beer,
If there's not, then there's none.

If it's blue, then it's grey,
If it's grey, then it snows,
If it snows, then he stays,
If it doesn't, then he goes.

I'd just put the last words onto the second verse when I heard the bushes rustle outside. The boys were making their way past. The gravel on the driveway slipped beneath their feet. When the window opened I trembled: when the first foot hit the floor I sighed: when their flashlights came on and the beams began to swing across the dank room I waited until I could smell the reinforcement on Baker's breath, then grinned and backed up the stairs ahead of them. I knew my way, and they, for all their plotting, did not.

I was already in the kitchen, crouched down behind a counter, while they were fumbling through the boiler room. Finally they reached the stairs, and when the door opened and Spot poked his head out, glanced around, and slipped into the room, with Baker creeping behind him and lastly Willie . . . careful . . . quiet—

Yaah! Yaah! I threw the light on and rose up from behind the counter with my hands open at my ears, waving my fingers, jumping up and down on my bare, slapping feet. Yaah! Yaah! my madcap hair flew up, my bruised red clown lips flapped in the light, and I pulled down a pair of saucepans that were hanging over the stove and began to bang them together until the whole kitchen seemed to crash down around them; and the three stopped and stood, shaking, and stared wide-eyed at my jack-o'-lantern smile as I heaved the dented metal at them. I heard a nice pop as one pot caught Spot square on the kneecap.

Baker started backwards as if a dog had leapt at his chest, and he slammed heavily into Willie, who was bringing up the rear, and who completed his short shadowy walk-on by falling backwards through the door he'd just passed through. His hand was still on the doorknob and the door shut behind him: I could hear a muffled thumping as he rolled down the stairs offstage, leaving my two friends to me—Yaah! They tried to push themselves through the wall and Spot dropped his flashlight, knocking it out. I turned off the light again, and the kitchen went black.

Jesus! Baker said in a high teary voice as I quietly slipped back. What the fuck was that? From his seat Spot made a mewling noise.

Arm in arm, they started hastily from the room, but the first door they found led to the pantry, and I heard the crash of shelving coming down upon their heads as they fumbled around. Out they came again, with a dozen boxes, noodles, sugar, cereal, rice, and two cans of soup preceding them across the moonlit floor before their feet. Spot was now in the lead, and he had the sense to head towards the basement door again.

They were going to get away, I knew; they were going to disappear back into the bottom of the house before I could bring them

128

down for good. But just as Spot reached the door it flew open, and Willie stood there and stared—and looming up behind him I could see the dark flash of a familiar figure with his arms thrust out, his thin legs braced against the post of the bannister: it was Jones: he thrust his head forward in a strange motion, then there was a beating in the darkness, and Willie fell back into the shadows again and disappeared, though this time the sound of his impact after the door slammed shut was considerably louder.

At that exact moment Holiday's silhouette appeared at the kitchen door; and I ducked into the shadows and out the back door just as he turned on the merciless light again, revealing his crimson-robed form, with a dull grey pistol in his right hand—which he incontinently let fire, and simultaneous with the snap of brass on burning gunpowder a blossom-filled bottle on the window sill broke.

All right! All right! squealed Spot.

From the attic window I watched as two cherry-top police cars appeared at the door a few minutes later. Spot and Baker were led away, cuffed shadows on the front lawn while the whole family, father, mother, Marian and Olivia, stood in a row like ducks and watched from the front porch. A moment later an ambulance arrived up the drive. As the corpsmen passed with their medical things I heard the largest duck quack: the three burglars had told some story about an enormous woman in the kitchen, just to rob him of his single-handed glory.

One of them would have no telling left. When the gurney reappeared it bore a large figure, supine on the canvas and covered with a plastic sheet: Willie had landed in the basement with such force that he had broken his neck, and he was dead.

13

The excitement made Olivia uneasy. I knew why; I could sense it on her thicker breath. What's more, I remembered certain vivid symptoms from one of my father's books: she held her arms protectively across her chest; and once pink flesh had begun to darken as the pigment collected; and her appetite had lost its shyness; and there was a powder-blue box that had gone untouched in her bathroom for six weeks. I think Anne might have suspected as well. She never asked, but she wouldn't leave the girl alone, wouldn't leave her to me, alone. She stopped by twice in one morning just before Labor Day weekend to check on Olivia; I was in her bathroom, having left her when I heard her mother knocking, and I was standing by an open window, ready to slip out and crawl silently down the side of the house. Do you need anything? Anne asked.

No, I'm okay. Soft, familiar voice.

How did you get this bruise here. She touched the purple flesh with the tips of two adjacent fingers.

I don't know, Olivia said. Where? She twisted her head to look at the shoulder that I had gently bitten the night before. I think, getting out of the shower.

Well, be careful. Oh— Mrs. Kelley stopped by this morning to see you, but you were still asleep. Kelley was her math teacher, an elderly woman I'd noticed only as she was leaving, and then just because she'd accidentally honked her horn. She says to say hello, and she hopes your whole summer isn't ruined.

No. That's nice.

I'm going to go into town. Are you sure you're all right?

Mmmm. Her mother stood up to leave. Mom, Olivia asked. Did Daddy come in to see me last night?

I don't know, her mother answered as she bent and stroked the girl's hair. She couldn't, since she and her husband had long since taken to different bedtimes; she went to sleep early so that she could be awake in the morning to see Marian off to school and make breakfast for Olivia, and he would stay up late, working in his study or watching television. They barely spoke, they had drifted into a sort of separation, and I was sure that her daughter's question wouldn't make it back to him.

It was well it wouldn't, because I couldn't let them have her, not an inch, not if I'd have gotten the world itself, and all its gardens and

130

girlfriends, never, never, never. You see, she was precious to me, and she was carrying something precious. I watched her carefully, watched them, I should say, but I never said a word, she had decided, and we shared an unspoken, astounding secret. She kept it to herself until several weeks later, when her mother found her vomiting in the bathroom one morning and immediately knew why. Olivia had hoped no one would notice until it was too late for anything to be done, and that was why she hadn't told them: the child, curled like a comma inside an O, belonged to my bride and me, and she had chosen to keep it.

14

Is she?
Yes.
Is she?
Yes, she is.
Olivia. It can't be.
It is.
A child?
A baby. You will be a grandfather.
She is, then. And winter coming. I see now how it goes. The days grow short and cold, and she delivers snow.

15

A storm immediately broke in the house, her father's thundering in the living room, her mother's face at his shoulder, overcast with clouds, her sister's sudden flashes of protectiveness. Marian wouldn't stop moving around, circling around him, speaking out from a spot next to a floor lamp, then from the doorway, then from a position she had taken up behind the couch where Olivia sat, her feet planted on the floor defiantly, her hands in her thick lap. Finally Holiday ordered her to settle down, and she sat in a chair in a corner.

No father could be found: when they asked her Olivia simply shook her head and bit her bottom lip. Holiday was utterly unprepared, and his helplessness left his mouth as fury. Was it Henry Bell! he shouted. Was it that blond-haired boy, what was his name! In the hallway closet I recoiled at the possibility—unknown until that moment—that her eye might ever have landed on someone else. Bellness and blondness, boyness, blondboyness immediately entered my vocabulary, though I never had an occasion to say them. Olivia lowered her head and shook it again. Well, this is fine, Holiday said suddenly.

Honey, why didn't you say something? Anne asked. You know we would have done everything we could to help.

Marian made a face that only Olivia and I saw. I thought of a cartoon cat and Olivia smiled despite herself.

This is funny? said Holiday. Marian started to laugh, Olivia laughed and looked away. The old man's face reddened: he made a noise like a racing engine and turned to his wife for help; her mouth was twisted, as if she were tasting lemon juice. No, she said, it isn't funny, really.

Holiday started to speak again, stopped, shook his head, and left the room. When he was gone the girls sighed and relaxed. I'm sorry, said Marian. I just, you know. I was nervous.

It's all right, said Anne. He's not going to get over this, you know. She was angry, although at whom I couldn't tell. She asked Marian to leave them alone for a few minutes, and when she was gone she took Olivia aside and pleaded, reasoned, reassured, but the girl wouldn't say, and finally she was allowed to return to her room, where she lay on her bed on top of the covers and—it was a scene she remembered from a movie—practiced breathing to relax. As the day closed her mother and her sister took turns visiting her, and it was impossible for me to see her, so I hid, hot-eared in the basement, until at last they retreated to bed, leaving her to me and my proud, pleased whispers.

I took her by the hand and brought her to the window onto the dark yard, and together we looked down at the long, wild paths and shoots, the bowers and glades; and as the trees shook in the wind, shadows slipped out from beneath the bushes to dance in the moonlight on the lawn, performing a wedding masque to faint, illegible strains of garden music. Now they spin in groups of two, now they bow and curtsy, now they dissolve into the darkness, only to appear at the edge of the pool of porch light to turn their faces up to where we stand and wish us well.

We went back to our bed and she lay on her back, her hands gently resting on her abdomen, as if she were coaxing the soft cells binding inside her. She said, Do you love me?

I said, So much. Do you love me?

You are perfect, she replied; then she suspired softly and turned onto her side, presenting me with her broad, moon-pale back, through which I could see her spine protruding like the skeleton of a snake. In a moment they were asleep.

16

I went to visit her father at his office one day soon after her pregnancy became a natural fact. I knew it was a dangerous thing to do, but I couldn't keep away; with his daughter's life now linked to mine by what we'd made together, the urgency of keeping her made me anxious to know as much as I could about his life and what he could do. So I called the number in Anne's phone book, and when his secretary answered I coolly told her that I was a local landlord looking for some legal advice. I gave my last name as Beech. How do you spell that? she asked. Like the tree, I said. There was a pause while she checked his appointments; I heard her inhale through her mouth. Well, Mr. Miller is very busy, she said at length. I won't be long, I replied.

That night I removed the page with my appointment on it from the leather-bound book he kept so that he'd be prepared for work each day, and the next morning I set off into town. It was a day so hot and bright that I could barely see, and the only life on the streets was a trio of black crows who followed me, circling and shouting comic insults. A half an hour earlier Olivia herself had left the house; out of her father's earshot her mother had taken her aside and, brushing her daughter's hair from her forehead with a quick stroke of her hand had said, I'm going to take you in to see my obstetrician today, okay? Olivia smiled shyly and nodded. Anne started the car and let the air-conditioning run for a few minutes before she returned to the house and retrieved the girl from her room.

Holiday's office was on the top two floors of a low office building near the courthouse in the center of town. I arrived at the proper hour, dressed in a new suit that I'd bought especially for the occasion. As I got off the elevator I noticed the firm's name painted on a pair of glass doors at the end of the corridor—Hunter, Tailor, Miller and Smith—as if hers was an ordinary sort of name and not the word I intended to change. In the reception area I found a black-haired woman with a thin, tense mouth who'd removed her shoes and sat with her tan-stockinged feet peeking out from beneath her desk. When I announced my name she invited me to take a seat and buzzed Holiday from the phone console before her. Beech, she said. No, Beech—like the tree. She looked down at the calendar on the desk before her and then glanced nervously up at me. He's here now, she said. (Pause.) Two-thirty. I have it right here. I heard a twittering from the receiver as his voice rose; she reddened in response, said Yes sir, and hung up the phone.

She ushered me into an empty conference room, handed me a cup of coffee, and left me to scan the shelves of law books. I quickly grew bored, and I'd picked up a coffee pot from the countertop that ringed the room and was idly peering into it—it was empty—when the door opened and the old man came in, puffed up, serious and sincere. At once I stared into his eyes to see if he started or some grimace took hold of him, but he barely saw me at all. He smiled; I smiled even more widely and got up from my seat to shake his hand. I'm sorry to keep you waiting, he said. He shook his head indulgently. My secretary is . . . .. His grasp was soft and formless, and I held his fingers a moment too long, so that a small ripple of discomfort passed over his face. Sit down, sit down, he said, doubling the greeting so that he had time to possess himself again. Do you want some more coffee? No, I said, and put the pot down again. He pulled a chair out from the head of the table and lowered himself into it; I sat at the opposite end.

He seemed to be intent on something at my chest, and I bent my head down to see what it might be, and then drew the ribbon of silk up with my hand and displayed it to him. He blinked. I'm sorry, he said. A nice tie you have there—and he unconsciously reached his hand up to straighten the knot in his own.

Thank you.

I have one just like it . . . somewhere, he said wistfully. Oh? I said, and gazed down at it again, my mouth pulled down in an involuntary frown. I got it from my father-in-law.

Married?

More or less, I said.

There was a moment while he pondered what I might have meant. Yes, he finally said, to break his own absorption. From that moment on he was officious and patronizing. Well, what can I do for you? he asked. You're too young to be in much trouble, eh? He smiled.

No, no, I assured him. At least, I hope not. I was given your number by George Fowler (a name I'd lifted off a document in his office one morning before sunrise). I was, I said, a child landlord, thanks to a sizable trust that I hinted might be his to manage if he helped me. I was trying hard to be responsible. But I had a tenant left over from the last owner who was holed up in one of the best rooms in the building, and I was losing money on the little rent I was collecting from her. Did I make her an old woman? I may have, though if I did it I was taking things foolishly far. I was riding a bigger horse than I could handle, and I wanted to see how high he'd jump. When he landed I was still on his back, but that was luck.

Of course, said Holiday when I was done. He unbuttoned his jacket, leaned back in his seat, smiled a fat yellow smile. This sort of thing happens all the time, you'll see. There's a lot . . .. Well. Here's what we can do. For the next few minutes he outlined a system of shameless paper harassment. He said he'd be happy to execute it for me, named a ridiculous hourly fee, and gave me an estimate of his time.

Is there anything else? he asked.

No. Thank you, I answered—although at the words my tongue nearly shriveled and fell from my mouth like a dead leaf. I'll call, I said as he showed me to the door. His parting handshake was firm. When I left him I felt filthy, and my appetite had crumbled like a mud bank in a flood.

17

Stubborn Holiday kept on claiming Olivia, his daughter, my bride. He didn't know who his rival was, or even that he still had one, a force tearing her out of his mean gravity, an enemy so close that I could tell when he passed by a hiding place I'd taken by the sweet smell of his tobacco. He spoke to Anne one night about convincing the girl to abort her pregnancy—he wondered if there wasn't some way to force her—while I shook helplessly in the closet in the hallway outside their room. Don't you dare! said Anne, furiously, quickly. You just keep away from her! Her cheeks went splotch red; they offset the white around her eyes, making her look feverish with some admirable ethic. No one was going touch her daughter's body or what it contained without the girl's consent—and her daughter had no intention of giving it up.

The summer had come to a close, and she wouldn't be going back to school, not in her condition. By then my beautiful wife's belly had grown slightly round, as if filling with the time and life the year was letting out, until it became a gentle curve, with the skin stretched tight over our baby; and our baby beat it from inside with its little fists, already restless and angry, a fierce child, the precarious mixture of a pair of lovers. At night I lay awake next to Mother Olivia, locked safely in her room with my arms wrapped around the two of them, and gave in to my huge happiness. When I slept it was as if there never was harm in the world. It's true I was the monster under the bed, the monster in the midnight closet, the very figure of a child's sleepless fears, but I think she felt more secure knowing that I was always near her, that the only desire I had was to protect her. She took to talking aloud while I was hiding, telling me of the baby's movements, considering names, and shamelessly, wittily bragging about

136

herself, her abilities, her body. I'm a mean machine, she whispered, and giggled redly. I'm the Queen of Sheba.

What about me?

You? You're just a . . . sperm thing. Could have been a turkey baster.

I made a hurt noise.

But you did very nicely. For a palace slave, and if you're good I'll let you live—if you service me. Write me a song, will you? She grasped my shoulder with both hands and rocked it. I want to hear it tomorrow.

By the next morning one was made. In it I fused the world as I knew it into a single word, which could be cracked open to reveal the world again, a menagerie, a republic: it could only be sung.

18

She began to talk to me even when I wasn't around, a change that made no difference to her parents, since they'd become accustomed to her speaking to creatures that they couldn't see: but it alarmed me. She believed that I was everywhere, and I tried to be. I would trail her as she went through the house, making eccentric, covert rings around her like a meteor making epicycles around a wandering planet, slipping into a hall closet, disguising myself as a coatrack, becoming a book on the shelf, crawling into a liquor bottle on the sideboard and watching her as she stood in the front hall and tried to decide whether to leave the house. Should I go out? she asked out loud, as if the house would fall down if she gave the wrong answer. What, honey? her mother answered from the living room, and in a moment she was no longer alone.

I knew she was uncomfortable, though she seldom complained. Night after night I felt her awake, rocking while I slept, a girl in a rowboat above a deep-sea diver. She would lie on her back and stare at the ceiling, her hands in fists at her side as she was moved by small, worrisome waves, waiting for a breeze and shifting restively from time to time. Just at dawn one day I awoke completely and rolled over to find her there. Hello, I whispered.

Hello.

You haven't slept all night.

Not really, no. She pulled herself up until she was leaning against the headboard.

How come?

I don't know.

Frightened?

Shhh. I don't know.

Would it be better if . . .

I don't know, she said patiently.

I lay my arm across her hips. Her skin was hot and moist.

I'm not frightened of, you know, no. It's just that I've been having these dreams. Last night, I mean the night before this one, I dreamt there were insects coming out of my mouth and my nose; the night before that my arms turned to legs, or they both, they were all like legs on a table. Before that I dreamt about a dog that spoke to me, but I don't know what it said. I knew in my dream, but when I woke up I couldn't remember. They make my days so slow and strange. She shook her head and slid back down onto the mattress, and when I said her name a minute later she didn't answer: she was asleep.

The next morning she was tired and temperamental. She burst into tears at any opportunity, and she made opportunities out of nothing. A fork dropped on the floor as she was fixing lunch was proof that the world was irreparably damaged: her mother found her sitting helplessly at the table a few minutes later, rocking back and forth and shaking, and when Olivia gestured to the fallen instrument she bent down, picked it up, put it in the dishwasher, and brought her another one—but by then she wasn't hungry.

At first I thought that she'd stumbled with the weight of her life and the one she carried, but as time passed and she grew worse instead of better, I began to be frightened for her; she seemed to be open to any influence, and it was impossible to tell what new fantasy might visit her next. She had a memory of me deep within her, but I think

138

she couldn't quite believe what she'd done; through the haze of her doubt she could see herself in short perspective, the plane of her own cheek with the expression of her eye trapped in the corner, a glimpse of her pale, soft leg from her knee to her thigh, a patch of scrub black hair. I was reminded of a painting I'd seem in a high-school art appreciation class of a broken pitcher on a table and a girl with a stricken look who watched from the shadows. I didn't leave the house, and she didn't give me up, but she often avoided me, and when she did agree to stay with me she would quickly become bored, and then her face would fall and she'd leave again, as if I were nothing but a magic lantern slide projected on her bedroom wall, a wavering, unfocused image traced in pallid flesh and grey tones. In the morning I would hear her vomiting in the bathroom, but she wouldn't let me in to hold her, and she wouldn't look at me, or talk to me, when she was done.

19

It was four in the morning and I'd awakened suddenly to discover her standing by the window looking into the backyard, a parabolic figure in a white nightdress, overlaid with blue harlequin shadows. Wilson, she said without turning around. There's sap running down the bark on the trees, it's thick and sticky. Sweet. I don't know how it happens. When it dries it gets hard and clear. That's sex. If I could wedge myself open wider, I could hold the world, and be safe from everything that was safe in me. That's sex, too. I can't do it.

Olivia. She came over to the bed and sat on the edge; I wrapped my arms around her and rocked her to sleep with a lullaby:

Sleep, my darling. Tears that burn
In young girls' eyes will always dry
With night's returning secrecy.
So the wisest child learns.
In my restful arms reserve
Thoughts of your most splendid hour:

Dreams that fix your passing powers,
High on love's unbreaking wave.

So she slept, and for a single night peace was restored, but verses couldn't contain her worries.

She began to lie to me. There were times when I couldn't follow her as she went from room to room, wandering in and out of her father's study, the living room, the kitchen. If her mother came upon her she would ask if she were looking for something.

Nope, Olivia would answer. Just looking.

She'd grow annoyed with me and slip away, joining her sister in her bedroom or lying half-undressed on a white wicker chaise in the sun on the back porch. One evening she left the house in a tight sundress and peddled unsteadily off to town on her bicycle, sick as she was. I tried to follow her, but by the time I'd snuck out to the road she was long gone, and there was no way for me to find her. I stood there on the shoulder, a golem in a grown man's suit under the dusk and street lamps, and kicked vainly at nothing, like a coyote caught in a trap. In time I gave up and went back to the dusty attic, where I waited with my fists clenched by a window, counting the cars that passed by the house, the minutes, the number of times I involuntarily trembled. Were those her footsteps on the gravel? It was a raccoon. My consciousness was jarred by the sounds outside like a loose tooth suffering a kernel of uncooked corn. Every second brought another hour of waiting.

When she returned at last I asked her where she'd been, but she wouldn't say, and when I wheedled and worried her for an answer she finally burst out and said, I went into town. I went to the library to read. I didn't believe her, but there was nothing I could do: I couldn't leave her, and I couldn't stand for her to lie to me. I suspected her of everything, of harboring unfair intentions, of longing to betray me, of secretly hating me.

Who are you yelling at? her mother asked through her door.

No one, said Olivia, looking too deliberately at me—and I was gone. Instead of coming to bed that night she sat with Marian in the

140

kitchen for an hour or two without me; I could see them at the table, under the light in the otherwise dark room, used tea things and a plate of cookies before them, making lazy talk, staring downwards.

20

She had always been an unselfconscious girl. I used sit on the edge of the bed and watch her get undressed each night. She took each piece of clothing off without moving from the spot where she stood: first she kicked off her shoes, then she bent like a crane to awkwardly remove her socks, then carelessly unbuttoned her jeans, pushing them roughly down her hips and stepping out of them. At last she pulled her shirt swiftly over her head and tossed it onto a chair. Then she would reach behind her, fingers twisting, remove her bra, and walk into the bathroom, bare but for the small cotton V curving down below the soft shelf of her abdomen. I loved to watch her go, swinging slightly on her footsteps. I admired her body's balance and obedience, the distribution of strengths to which it testified; it seemed to be carved out of a single generous piece of rose-white material, yielding nothing to its parts. Sometimes I would wonder what it would be like to live in it, and more than once I caught myself inadvertently imitating her proud walk, imagining breasts below my shoulders, a soft, short waist, a heaviness in my hips, the difference between my legs; and I would blush with curious excitement.

As she passed by me one night I noticed that she'd drawn on the flesh of her forearms with a marker, a mapway of arrows and circles and tiny symbols that she'd invented, using her body as if it were paper. I put my hand out and stopped her. Olivia? I asked. She didn't speak, but she sat down on the edge of the bed beside me and held her arms out, overturned so that the smooth flesh on the underside of her arms showed. The marks made sentences up to her bare shoulders. There's more, she said, and with that she lay gently back on the bed with her legs dangling off the mattress, and spread her knees as if she were opening the leaves of a rare book. On the skin of her pale thighs, just below her dark, silent mouth there were more marks, but I couldn't read them; whatever code they might have contained was as closed to me as a paragraph of Arabic. Okay? she asked, and I shook my head. She frowned as if she were disappointed in me and went into the bathroom.

She decided that her medium was insufficient. By the next night the ink had been washed away. It was replaced by dried blood: she'd carved thin, painstaking cuts in her flesh, again on the tenderest lining of her arms and thighs. The ideograms were forgotten; the pink welts appeared in ragged and uneven rows, in one case a group of four intersected by a diagonal fifth, like a crude counting habit. When I asked her what she wanted to say she just showed the angry scars she'd inscribed and looked away. I took her wrists in my hands and searched her countenance for a reason, but I couldn't find one.

21

Strings snap on the blue guitar. Explorers fail to reach their mark and expire nowhere. Glamour ends its happy visit, and in the eyes of the one I loved I found a fish's lidless stare.

22

Late the next night I woke suddenly and found myself rafting alone in the darkness, the mattress empty beside me. The blanket was still warm from her body, still sweet from her perfume. The floor was covered with a cool, soft mist; it lapped silently at the edge of the bed. On her desk across the room I saw the luminous red glow of her alarm clock, and as I watched, wondering what the numbers meant, the last digit changed from eight to nine. I heard a movement in the bathroom, a kind of sigh. I heard it again. So I got up, shivering, to see. Olivia was sitting on the sink in her dark bathroom, with thin white shards of a light bulb scattered on the tile floor and a fragment of the glass between her fingers. When she heard me enter she looked up; I was yawning, I wasn't thinking of yawning. It was air into the manifold, and it propelled me across the tiles. I caught her soft sweaty hand in mine, yanking it to one side and prying it open until the glass fell: immediately she slapped my face with her other hand, pulled away, and pressed herself against the tiled wall in the far corner by the door. You took advantage of me, she said, her eyes filled with angry tears. You know you did. She opened her arms: And it hurts. My father is going to kill you. He's going to kill both of us. She panted for breath.

Every language has the worst five words, and everyone who has heard them was the first. Just then, as playground swings made silent arcs in the darkness, and waitresses held coffee pots above sleepless customers' cups, and traffic lights turned red on empty roads, she abruptly became calm and spoke them to me as if she were reporting bad economic news. Anyway, I don't love you anymore, she said. I wish you would leave.

I didn't ask her why, because I didn't believe her—it seemed like one of those sentences (all lovers are always liars) that couldn't possibly be true. She might as well have tried to convince me that I didn't exist, this best boy whom my love had made; it was like standing in front of a mirror and seeing nothing but the room reflected. I was suddenly very tired, exhausted really; my skin hung from my body as heavily as a wet robe. So I frowned, turned away, and went to my mattress in the basement, where I slept as innocently as a puppy. A few lost hours later I was awakened by Olivia herself. Wilson, Wilson, she said. There you are. I could feel her crawling in beside me. God, I looked all over. Don't listen to me when I talk like that, Okay? she said as she put her arms around me from behind.

23

She wore long-sleeved shirts while she healed, but her mother discovered the fading scars on the skin of her arms one night when she came in to tuck the girl into bed. I listened through a wall as she told Holiday about it a few minutes later. He came in to see her afterwards but by then she was feigning sleep, and when he said her name from the threshold of her room she didn't answer. The next morning he stopped in on his way to work and tried again, but she was in the bathroom and wouldn't come out, and he couldn't bring himself to try once more.

That night there was a final summer storm, a full hour of thunder striking against the window, and clouds that dumped buckets of water onto the roof. Olivia slept through the night. I stood by the window and watched the wind bend the trees, turning the leaves into dark, violent spumes. Spouts of rain whirled through the grounds, casting themselves against the pane until it shook in its frame. A wicker chair that someone had forgotten to bring inside tumbled off the patio, came to a stop, underwent a crazy shiver, and then rolled end over end into the darkness. As I followed it my eyes landed on a faint form at the edge of the black into which it had disappeared.

He was standing in his torn coat, his hair hanging in wet mopstrings; I couldn't see his face, but I recognized his stance, and the quick, birdlike movements he made as he whipped the water up with his arms: it was Jones, come again to cure her. Suddenly the sky lowered to the eaves like the lid of a box; and the house, long since asleep, was engulfed by waves. There was the hiss of eddies foaming as they broke against the walls, and the casements began to rattle. The trees swayed like seaweed. I could see him swimming on the lawn, treading water as if he were slow-dancing in the downpour. After a few minutes he turned his back and started for the bottom of the garden.

A moment later I heard Holiday urgently calling his wife from the bottom of the stairs. Anne! he shouted. Anne! There was no answer. Olivia slept soundly, peacefully, her mouth slightly open, her fingers curled into a loose fist at her ear, as if she were holding a ladybug that she wanted neither to crush nor to let escape. Anne! I heard their bedroom door open and Anne's slow footsteps on the landing. Shhh! she said sleepily. What is it?

Call the police, right now.

What is it? she asked again. By then he was halfway up the stairs, and through a crack in the door I saw him holding his pistol loosely in his right hand, with its barrel pointed towards the ground. What are you doing? she said. He wore the look of a man who's just come, glassy-eyed, unthinking, and oddly helpless.

It happened again, he said quietly. I missed. Call the police, will you? Already? No, wait. I'd better call my office. What time is it?

It's two in the morning.

I'm all right, he said. But where's my phone book? I'd better call someone at home. There was, I shot at someone in the back yard. Anne started to put her hand up to her face, and then stopped, as if she were embarrassed by the gesture. She looked briefly at his gun-gripping hand as he reached the landing, and then looked away. For his part, he seemed to have forgotten about the weapon; he left it on a night table in the hallway as he passed into their bedroom to use the phone, though just before he shut the door he turned, waved at it shortly, and said, He ran away.

The police arrived some minutes later, and Holiday gave his story to them, in competition with their radios, which spat and called constantly. In time they left, taking the gun along with them to pass a perfunctory examination. It was returned to Holiday a few days later; it was legal and registered. The intruder was never found.

24

When Olivia awoke the next morning the sky was clear and bright, and gleamed like just washed glass. She looked at me with clear, bright eyes and right away I knew that she was better, that her brittle, unbearable panic had washed away. I wanted her to stay with me for a few minutes, but she hopped up from her bed, threw some clothes on, splashed water on her face, and left me with a longish, warm kiss. Smooch, she said, and then left the room.

It was a Saturday, and though it was late in the morning her parents were still home; Holiday was recovering in his study, and Anne was cooking in the kitchen. She went to the kitchen first, marching through the door the way a schoolgirl enters her favorite class. Mom, she said. I feel much better. Is it too late for breakfast? Her mother, who'd been facing the sink, nearly jumped out of her shoes. She turned around swiftly and stood with her back against the porcelain, unconsciously wiping her soapy hands on her apron as she stared intently in Olivia's eyes. Yes, it was true. She could see it in the girl's familiar posture, in her half smile, as if she were waiting for something funny to happen: in fact she laughed at her mother's surprised silence. Then, and still smiling, she walked over to the dishwasher, removed a clean glass, went to the refrigerator, and poured herself some orange juice, which she drank in two long, throat-pulsing gulps. The remains of her smile still showed in the corners of her mouth, and some of the juice spilled onto her chin. She wiped it away with the bottom of her T-shirt, pulling it up far enough to expose both her distended belly—her bloodless white navel protruded slightly—and the lower part of a black lace bra.

Olivia, her mother said, and then crossed the linoleum floor and stood before her with her hands on her shoulders as if to steady her before her eyes. Honey. I'm so glad to see you better. Are you really? The girl nodded confidently. I want to take you to the doctor this afternoon.

All right, Olivia replied. Can I have some breakfast first?

When she had finished eating Anne came and sat across the table from her and carefully explained what had happened the night before. I don't want you to worry, she said. Daddy will be just fine, and no one's going to get in here. When Olivia came back to her room I could see that she was trying to decide what to make of it—I'd never told her about Jones; I was afraid she would think I was crazy. She said nothing to me. Instead, she took a shower and changed her clothes, and then she returned to the living room to wait for her mother. Anne was taking her time dressing. Olivia started to walk onto the back porch, only to discover Holiday standing a few yards into the back lawn, staring at the bottom of the garden. She stopped,

146

staggered, feinted once to her left as if she hoped to head around the corner before he spotted her, and then backed into the house again. At the sound of the door closing behind her he turned, blinking questioningly.

With a blank look she walked quickly through the house, opened the front door, stuck her head out, looked carefully around, and then sat down on the front steps. A few minutes later Anne found her: Oh, there you are, she said as she searched through her purse for her car keys. I was waiting for you inside. Sorry, said Olivia.

Through the windshield of the car I saw Anne turned as far around in her seat as she could as she steered the car backwards down the driveway and out onto the street. Her arm was cast out on the seat back behind Olivia's head; her daughter sat with her hands in her lap and looked straight ahead, unblinking, watching the receding, sunlit house.

Anne dropped her off later that afternoon and then left again, and Olivia virtually ran to her room as soon as she was through the door. I was waiting for her; she pulled the shades and sat down on the edge of her bed, her arms folded across her belly. The last sunlight was pushing weakly through the treetops: Olivia? Marian shouted from the bottom of the stairs. Do you want some of this cake I made?

No, thank you! to the door. The doctor says the baby is fine, to me, her eyes shining in the darkened room. Do I want to know if it's a boy or a girl?

Do we?

Oh, I don't know, she said. I don't think so.

No, I said. Let's not.

. . . .

Olivia, are you really okay?

Of course, she said, looking away as she patted my knee with one hand. I'm just worried about a friend of mine. The remainder of the day was given to Marian, who dragged her sister out of the house and took her for a long, intimate walk, down the hill to the foot of the driveway, down to the end of the block, and then out of sight.

25

She managed to last an entire week without having to be alone with her father. She was at the dinner table every night, and he sat at the head, but she never looked at him, and he never spoke to her. Only once in the following week did he address her: he asked her what she was planning to do about school.

Marian immediately said, Nothing right now. Her gunmetal voice took Holiday by surprise, and he turned to face her angrily.

Who are you? he said to her.

She's not going to do anything, she doesn't have to worry about that right now.

Who are you? Marian didn't say anything. I'm talking to you, he said, and his voice grew louder.

Stop it, said Olivia, her eyes wide with supplication. The table immediately fell silent, and as if to take the attention off like a robe she got to her feet and began to clear the dishes. As she passed her father on her way to the kitchen he suddenly reached out and took hold of her shirt in his fist. He held her; his knuckles brushed her belly. She froze and stared at the stack of plates in her hands.

You are not my daughter, he said.

26

The music that I mentioned at the very start had already begun an unnerving melody, and it soon became martial.

Holiday chose one night that week to announce to Marian at the end of dinner that he'd been offered a new job with another firm in California. He and Anne had already discussed it, and he was considering it. The family, of course, would have to move. The tone of his voice suggested that he intended to make his decision based on what, by his own lights, would be best and most reasonable, and he seemed genuinely surprised at the pall that fell over the table when he'd finished. A wet magnolia sprig blew against the dining room window, the twig clicking against the glass before it fell rapidly out of sight.

What about school? Marian finally asked, her eyes wide in her suddenly bloodless face.

What about it? he answered.

I only have one year left—

There are schools there, you know, he said, as if, with a disappointment so personal as to be almost unspeakable, he was telling her something that she didn't know.

Honey . . . said her mother.

But all my friends, said Marian.

You'll make new friends, said Holiday. Marian reddened, bent her head, and struggled with herself. Holiday waited patiently for her to cry. It was close. She picked up a fork in her fist and made two quick movements towards her plate. I expected her to lunge at him with it next. Her mother flinched. Anyway, Anne said hastily, it's not for certain.

But if it is . . . Holiday threatened.

Marian pushed her chair back and got up. We're not done with dinner, said Holiday. I am, she answered, and walked quickly from the room while he said her name like an order to her back. As she disappeared through the doorway he rose from his seat and started after her, only to stop again and call instead: Don't you dare say anything to Olivia.

As Marian's footsteps started up the stairs he returned to his seat at the head of the table. When he picked up his knife and fork again he had them in the wrong hands, and he spent a few seconds trying to exchange both of them at once—but his hands began to shake and he quickly gave up and set them down on his plate again.

That was nice, said Anne. He stared at her, and as he stared he grew elephantine, and leaned his big body over the table to trumpet. Why don't you decide, then? he said. You and Marian! Oh, and Olivia, why don't the three of you decide where I should work, and then tell me?

That's not the point, she said.

What is the point? What is the point? Florid, a flush-faced ele-phant, wallowing and thrashing around.

Anne became a stubborn bird, perched out of reach. She's upset that she might have to leave just when she was starting to get along . . .

Besides, it'll be better for Olivia to get away from here. And he pulled his head around, ears inertially flapping, and lumbered away.

27

From that night on my life with Olivia was losing her. It was like trying to watch a television with the vertical out of adjustment; it was always the first moment that she was drifting away, starting off again, starting again; but she was never gone. All her confidences went into her sister's pocket; as often as not a day spent in mutually secretive company—when they were together it was as if each one knew, even with her back turned, the precise location and attitude of the other—would end with her sleeping in the extra bed in Marian's room while I lay alone in the basement.

As her body continued to change, her ankles swelling, her hips thickening, her breasts becoming heavier, she became elusive; she went to some place where I couldn't find her, though I was the one who had put her there. When she saw me she treated me as if I were a friend who happened to stop by to see her. Oh, hello, she'd say, slightly surprised to find me in front of her; and then she'd be cheerful and friendly, in a somewhat distant way, until she'd abruptly mention that she had to go off and do something vaguely described, and she'd leave me again. If I tried to follow she would turn and stare at me as if she couldn't believe I would be so inconsiderate.

She disrupted the rhythm of my reason with the thousand deci-sions a frightened lover makes—here I find her, after midnight, and she's asleep without me. Is it better to risk annoying her by waking her, or should I sit by the window, and painfully wonder what she dreams? If I confess with a hundred pleas and a hundred kisses, will she grow disgusted or ashamed and turn away? Every moment that she spends in the privacy of her senses is a moment away from me. She'll forget me, she doesn't care. I'll go crazy: I'll run to the river and throw myself in, and sink until the weeds wrap around my head.

She spent three consecutive nights in Marian's room. On the morning of the fourth day I waited for her in her room. When she came in she seemed slightly confused by my being there; she blinked a few times and unconsciously rubbed her upper arm, bunching her T-shirt up to her white, round shoulder. Sit down beside me, will you? I said. She frowned at the floor; she gently kicked her toe against the leg of the bed.

Listen, honey . . . she said. I stared at her. She wrapped her hands around the bedposts as if she were grasping the ropes of a swing, and swayed slightly over the mattress. Listen, things are getting all fucked up around here.

I heard, I said. I won't let them move.

I know, she said, leaning as far backwards as she could. But I don't want anything to happen. Can . . .? I'm sorry. My heart began to hammer in my chest, and patches of my skin began to unstitch. Can you, I think it would be best if you went away for a while, because everything has to be normal around here, and— Oh, honey, she said, as I shook my head to put out the sudden scraps of burning paper that had started to curl in the corners of my thoughts. They wouldn't die, so I rose to my feet and started for her bathroom; I couldn't find the door. She was standing at the foot of the bed watching me as I turned around again; she was actually wringing her hands. I've thought about this so much, she said. Please, just until the baby is born. Please?

I turned and said, No, Olivia. I can't leave now.

No? But you have to.

Why?

Because I want you to, she said firmly. Because you can't stay. I'm asking you, because I need you to go now.

Where can I go?

I don't know, go to Colorado, go to California, and when you come back you can tell me all about it. Save some money and when you get back everything will be fine, I promise. Please.

Her voice had taken on an excited tone, but I could tell she'd forced it for my benefit; it was theatrical and false. I'd never known her to turn a feeling into an effect, and I took it as a terrible sign, and shuddered inwardly at her tepid smile.

I want you to leave, she said. I could feel a cherub watching on over my shoulder, her roseate face downcast in grief; it was like a weight.

The baby, I said.

What about it.

I reached out my hand to her and she recoiled.

Don't! she said.

I took a step towards her. I just want—

Don't touch me! she said, and threw her arms up protectively, grimacing as if the thought of my putting my hands on her would cause her skin to shed like a snake's. You're crazy, and you have no right to hurt me. Go away!

She stared at me, terrified; I stared at her, shocked, and then began to shake uncontrollably; my legs trembled, my mouth trembled, I couldn't find a place to keep my hands. There was no one else ever made but her, the rest were mechanical things in painted masks, but she was afraid of me. She backed to the door and my eyes dissolved, and when she turned around and ran from the room I began to sob, redly, brokenly, furiously, uncontrollably. At that moment I hated everything, and wanted to end the world, and everyone in it.

28

The next four months went by in a shallow succession of odd jobs, cold rooms, and unfriendly faces, overlaid in my mind like scenes on pallid acetate. I tended bar for a week in Shreveport, and rented a room in a cheap motel called the Regency, where I slept on a mattress no thicker than its blanket. In Tulsa I unloaded gunnysacks from trucks and slept in a shelter in the basement of a Baptist church. I was a waiter in a Wichita hotel—Heartbreak, said the manager when he hired me, gesturing across the lobby to the black-clad door-man and weeping bellhop—and went home every night to my car, parked in an alley off Lonely Street.

You may remember that as a particularly cold winter; I remember it as a gradual fading of the countryside's color as I moved north, until some limit of blankness was reached, and then I met a succession of indistinguishable white days, a bareness as still and silent as an empty house, white lights, white walls, white sky, white freeze spread across the land. The sky was an idea of a sky, unbroken and impossible to compass; it was weather as the number zero.

And then as if from its very fragility the sky cracked one afternoon like the ice on a pond and the snow began, and the world became whiter still. I was trapped in my car in a storm on a highway outside Oklahoma City, peering through the windshield as I passed mile after mile of semis that had slipped off the road and fallen over into ditches, where they lay toppled and broken like great animals. There was no sound. I kept on and made it as far west as Colorado; for a week I stayed in a small town in the sky outside Denver, where with my last thirty dollars I rented a room and drank my dinner. In a bar late that night I watched intently as a man beside me drew a deep drag on his cigar, formed his mouth and locked down with his jaw, blowing a casual smoke ring across the room, a giant, soft O that wavered and expanded for a few full minutes, inescapable vowel, grey in the pale grey air.

A little bit later I was in the bathroom—then by the bright juke-box, with someone to my left in blue jeans and boots—then at the bar, looking for my room key, or my gloves, or my glasses, except I had no glasses—and trying to say something to somebody—then out the front door in the cold air, stars like white needles above the dark pines. Down below Tupelo, sang a song behind the door, and suddenly I was digging for it with my teeth, not fallen, I realized, but pushed—I heard something hit my head, and then I was on the ground in the parking lot, with gravel in my mouth and a dull grey lead billiard ball bouncing around inside my skull, and then someone was kicking my back and my legs, over and over again. I woke up the next morning in my room, with blood on my pillow from the root of a lost tooth, a crack in my cheekbone with a swollen blood-purple bruise over it, and a limp that lasted a week and a half.

I sold the Ford for two hundred dollars so that I could afford to stay out of the weather. When the tracks cleared I went south by train to El Paso, sleeping in my seat as the wide ranches passed; then east again to the hills of Austin. There I tried to rob a car parts store south of the river; I waved a toy gun at the clerk and took one hundred dollars from the till, and I ran. I was standing in a shopping center parking lot ten minutes later when the police pulled up. The judge gave me six months in juvenile detention; I was told I would serve thirty days.

Locked up, I learned nothing, I saw no one. If I spoke more than five words in a day it was because someone hadn't heard me the first time. Every moment I had Olivia and my child in mind, and this was the song that I sang to my bars and bunk:

> Long time!
> I hate it here
> Cold time!
> Get me out of here.

I counted every day, at night I dreamed of bicycles and skating rinks, volumes of rhyming verse and white bedrooms. I got out on Christmas Eve. The New Year passed, and I knew the day of her delivery was nearing; so I made my way slowly back to her again. I was wondering all the while what I wanted, but I had been patient, I had been good, and I was going to go home to find what was left for me. I waltzed across Texas, alone, rolled through Louisiana like a roulette wheel, stopped briefly at the bridge to take a gander at the river and catch my breath, and then ran the rest of the way. And so it was that on the evening of the fifth of February I found myself at the cold side of their backyard.

154

29

The garden had long since gone into winter remission, but nothing else had changed. I don't know why I thought it might, but I was a little surprised as I rounded the bend in the road before the house and saw it come into familiar view. Like a musician stepping back into a song after leaving the stage, I felt oddly out of time, and I wondered if the music would still match.

It was dark in the amethyst light just after sundown; no lights burned in the windows. The trees were leafless, so I had some trouble finding a spot from which I could peer in through a window, but I chanced cover from a thick tangle of shrubbery outside the kitchen. The room inside was empty and dark, but everything was in place; the pots were still hanging from their hooks, and there was a bottle of olive oil left out on a counter, and a few dishes washed and safely placed in the drying rack beside the sink. Through the open kitchen door I could see into the living room. On the far wall was a mirror, almost fifty feet away, and my own face stared back at double the distance, framed by the mirror's edges, the doorway, the window, looking emptily into the vacant house. As if for the first time—as nervously as the first time—I found my window and crawled in. The boiler was on, murmuring with hot water. Otherwise it was the same.

At ten that night I saw the headlights from their car sweep across the scrim of the curtains in the living room, making shadows swing prophetically inside the room. I was hiding in the darkness at the top of the stairs; I heard a pair of car doors shut and footsteps on the walk; then the front door of the house opened and Holiday and Anne came in. Under the foyer light their faces were drawn with fleshly shadows; they looked a full five years older, and they were alone. Olivia and her sister had gone to the movies, or out to meet with friends, or down to school for some evening event, a play, a cotillion, a basketball game.

Holiday removed his coat and hung it in the closet in the front hall; then, without a word, he started slowly up the stairs to bed.

Anne went into the living room and turned on a light, sighed, and sat back on the couch without removing her outer things.

She'd just brushed her hair back wearily from her forehead for the tenth time when I heard a key in the lock, and my crouched breath began to quiver with excitement: I was home again, and soon I'd be reunited with Olivia. My mouth went dry, and my legs shook as the door opened.

Immediately, Marian came in and looked quickly into the living room, and I studied the darkness outside the door for the shadow of my wife, stared without blinking into the sliver of bright black framed by the white-painted pillars of the portico and swiftly diminishing under a contracting arc as the door found its way back into its frame. By the time I realized that Marian was alone she'd joined her mother in the living room. I heard them murmur to each other, daughter once, mother once, daughter again. Then the light in the living room went out and they started up the stairs to bed, and right away I knew that Olivia wasn't coming home, after all.

Sister

1

I spent three days trying to discover where she'd gone, but I learned nothing. It was a defeated house, the kind of house in which no voice is ever raised, and the corners of the rooms get uncommon scrutiny. Holiday and Anne would retire to the living room immediately after their silent dinner, where they'd sit before the television and slowly sip at benumbing drinks, he reclined in one corner of the couch, she upright in the other, in a room so mercilessly quiet that it was all I could do to keep from delivering my goddamns and bringing the roof down around them. When they'd had enough and rose from their positions at the end of the night neither of them would bother to bend down again to straighten the cushions that their weight had slightly dislodged: he walked slowly up the stairs, while she collected the glasses, took them into the kitchen, rinsed them halfheartedly, and left them in the drying rack, dawdling by the sink so that she could be sure he was in bed, with the lights out, before she reached the bedroom.

Marian ate her dinner alone in her room, and brought the dishes down to the kitchen by the back stairs when she knew her parents were settled in front of the television. Nearly everything else she did was a secret: her door was always shut; her book bag never left her side; phone calls to friends were whispered into the mouthpiece. Soon after dinner she would leave the house, and she wouldn't be back until late.

No one argued with her, and no one but me was ever awake when she came home. So I was the only one who noticed when, the night after I'd returned, she entered the house, hung her coat in the hall, and went into the kitchen. She took an apple from a lower drawer of the refrigerator and then sat at the table in the dark for ten minutes, chewing each mouthful deliberately. When she was done she threw the core away and headed to the dining room, from the dining room to the living room, from the living room to her father's office. She shut herself in, and a light silently appeared beneath the door. She was sequestered there for some time—the white moon rose an inch or two up the sky outside the window where I waited—but I couldn't tell if she'd found what she was looking for by the expression on her face when at last she emerged.

After she'd gone to sleep I let myself inside Olivia's door. Her furniture had not been touched, and each object had been left in place, but the room was as empty as any I had ever entered. As I passed by the foot of her bed I suddenly felt her hands on me, her palms on my back, her hips against my leg; the veins beneath my skin dilated, and I stopped and stretched my shoulders towards the feeling to make it last. It was a fool's memory, it was pyrite: she was long gone. A creak in the hallway made me start, and I quickly stood and headed for her bathroom, but it was just the house making tics as it slept, and when I was sure I was safe I went back and stood next to her bureau. The door to her closet was slightly ajar; there was a shoe protruding from the darkness, which had prevented it from closing completely. I nudged it back through the frame with my toe and pressed the door shut. Then I crossed the room and sat at her desk. Her red fountain pen was lying diagonally across the surface. The drawer was empty of everything but a pencil stub, a paper clip, and a two-page math exercise upon which a teacher had written a red Very Good next to a red 87. There was no note. I went through her closet, dividing the soft shirts on the hangers with my hands and peering into the corners; I dug through her dresser drawers, I checked the medicine cabinet in her bathroom, I looked under her bed. There was no clue.

I was careful to avoid her room from then on, though I was tempted to it like a drunk to a full tumbler; I could feel the flesh in my arms and legs dissolving, the string of my sinews coming undone; there was no relief for the numbness in my neck; and every surface that I touched was dull, was lifeless, loveless, and unpleasant, because nothing fit my hand and soothed the nerves there, and spread a flush throughout my body, as she had. I felt like a shadow casting a man. I would stop suddenly at a spot where I'd seen her, my only piece of the world, as she sat on the stairs the night of their party—or in the kitchen I'd find myself gazing endlessly at the tray upon which her dinner had been carried to her, now hung by one corner by a hook on the wall—or driven in by Anne on her way to the bathroom I would stand in the practice room by the flank of the grand piano she used to play, while the mocking sound of movie music drifted in from the living room.

From an upper window I watched as Holiday stood heavily in the dooryard one afternoon; I heard him mumbling to himself about the mess made of his grounds. Over there, he said to no one in particular, there was a yellow dogwood. Now there's . . . I don't know . . . I don't know what that is there. In fact it was all trash by then, fatuous litter. I could stir it with my hands and come up with nothing but debris. It wasn't just winter that had done it; no one had cared for it in months. Spring was coming, but no effort would be made to begin it again; it counted for nothing.

Everything counted for nothing, and I became convinced that the house without Olivia was actually empty, its characters cartoons, one step removed from the real, like insubstantial shades in hell. It was the latest of nights when I was reminded that it wasn't empty at all. I was reminded because I was found out, and I was found out because I was careless.

2

It was the third night after I'd come back; I think it was near dawn. I'd woken from my sleep to the hum of the basement and a darkness so deep and clear that it was like black water, and for a moment after my eyes opened I was uncertain that they had. But I could feel my heart beating in my chest, unaltered by the figures of dreams, so I decided that I was awake, and I sat up in my bed, allowing the covers to fall to my waist. I could hear the house breathing in around me, breathing out, counting the strikes of its architectural rhythm. I followed that breath with my own, a mirror of my mise-en-scene, and when I'd collected enough of myself I got up, pulled on my clothes, and slipped up the stairs to the kitchen, with the light from a far streetlight a faint illumination through the window; it was sufficient for me to glance down and see my hands, and remind myself that once I'd been determined to come into my agency.

I wanted breakfast so I went to the refrigerator, stuck my head in, and started to rummage through the dishes. Soon enough I found something in a plastic bowl, found a fork in a drawer, found a space by the sink, and I was standing in the darkness with my back against the countertop, picking at a casserole when my tongue suddenly went dead; it was as if my mouth were filled with sand and gravel. I couldn't hear, there were imaginary bells going off in the kitchen like a fire alarm: I couldn't feel the bowl in my hands: I couldn't make out a single word of my own thoughts through the din. But I could see, because the room was suddenly flooded with light.

She stood in the doorway with her legs planted and spread until her feet touched the corners of the frame; she wore a grey- and white-striped jersey, a blue-black skirt, and black leggings. One hand was propped up on the jamb while the other held her blue down jacket at her side. Her hair was swept back, exposing her wide, pale forehead. She was so utterly composed that it was as if some capricious sculptor had built her there years ago to hold the house up. She had a strange smile on her lips, but her eyes were dark and tired. She'd just come home.

It was a game to see who would speak first, and I was going to lose; I knew I was before the first few seconds were out, but I pushed my exclamations into my pocket. They started to escape: I pushed them back again, and held them down with my hand while they squirmed and struggled. Through it all she stood and watched me, just once raising a hand to her forehead to brush back a piece of hair that had fallen over her eyes. Oh, I finally said.

It wasn't enough to draw a response, so I said Oh again. My name is Wilson.

I know, said Marian. When did you get back?

The day before yesterday, I answered without thinking, though I caught myself quickly enough to clip the last vowel.

What will you do now that Olivia is gone?

I suppose my face might have fallen. I know I looked at the ground, trying to hide from her small, metallic gaze. I hoped that if

I waited long enough she might simply dissolve through the kitchen door again, but she seemed perfectly unconcerned with my silence, as if she had her hand on me and had allowed me to hide behind my speechlessness only because she saw no need as yet to make me twitch or jump with words. She let a few long seconds pass that way. What are you going to do now? she asked again.

I don't know.

Nice suit, she said, as deadpan as a hanging judge. Reminds me of one of my dad's. She furrowed her brow. A little ragged though. What are you going to do?

I don't know, I said. Please, will you tell me what happened? Where is she? I'll go.

Go where?

I don't know.

She came out of the doorway, walked across the kitchen floor, and dropped her jacket on the table. Then she drew a chair out and sat backwards in it with her chest pressed against the wooden top. Casting her bare arms out on the table in front of her, she pulled a few crumbs along in a wide arc with the tip of one delicate finger and then brought it up and absently crushed them against her thumb. She looked up at me again. What are we going to do?

Do, I don't know. Where is she?

She's gone. She stared at me, and after a moment or two had passed she said, I suppose I have to tell you.

I'll go as soon as I know, I said. I promise.

She spoke quietly and with perfect calm, and I've forgotten almost every word she used. Within a minute I had lost her voice. But I didn't miss a motion of the story she told: I can still wring out every moment, and arrange them in a rude order of reasons.

3

Olivia had been well enough for a week or two after I left; Marian had watched her carefully to be sure. Still, she wouldn't talk to her father, or even look at him. She ate her dinner quickly, without glancing down to the end of the table, and when she was done she would cross her knife and fork on the plate, and wait patiently to be excused. Marian enfolded her in a circle of her own friends, and with her sister's help she was out of the house as often as possible. Once or twice Holiday knocked on the door of her bedroom late at night, but she knew it was him and she wouldn't answer.

Anne was unnerved by Olivia's silence and evasiveness. One evening after Holiday had retired to his office she tried to explain his behavior, but when Olivia went grey and silent and refused to look up she grew embarrassed and stopped. He wasn't mentioned anymore.

It had been some time since he'd stopped asking her for the name of the baby's father, but instead of letting it pass he began to conduct an investigation of his own. He tried to be quiet about it, but it was like trying to tiptoe through a flock of sitting swans; every move he made ended in an explosion of outraged cries. In response a tone of mixed deviousness and brutality attached to his efforts. He called her home-room teacher from the year before and asked her to come by his office. There he asked questions for an hour, and when her teacher, who knew nothing, grew tired of knowing nothing and tried to leave, he suddenly lost his temper and began yelling at the bewildered woman. When Olivia found out, she cried to Marian, Marian went to her mother, and her mother told Holiday he should be ashamed.

The garden was dead, and worse, scarred by an incomplete effort that he'd made to reshape it in midwinter; a pile of desiccated rose bushes lay stacked against the foot of the house, and the herb garden was a shallow, angry hole that he had made with a spade. He went through her drawers one day when she'd gone to the doctor for her weekly checkup. He was looking for a letter, a name, an answer. He did find one extraordinary article, but it stole more meaning than it offered. He took it anyway.

When Olivia came home she noticed at once that her things had been moved; she confronted him in his study and begged him to leave her alone. He responded by yelling at her. Get out of here! he shouted. Get out of my house! Olivia ran from the room in tears just as Anne reached the door; Holiday turned his anger on his wife. It was Marian's fault anyway. Olivia must have gotten the idea somewhere, it must have been her sister. He knew something like this would happen, he announced. The girls could not be trusted.

She waited until he was done and then left the room without saying a word.

Then Holiday enlisted a doctor; Olivia wouldn't confess to him. He suggested a therapist, but she wouldn't go. Boarding school was mentioned; she refused to be threatened. Still she was coming apart. As she became convinced that her father hated her and wanted to hurt her she weakened, and for the first time she was frightened of the seriousness she faced.

She worried about love, and wondered where I was. She was angry with me. She had just one thing to remember me by, and it was huge and hurt.

Then she began to save things; it was strange. Her room became a reliquary for everything she used, no matter how disposable it was meant to be, everything, scraps of paper, peach pits, bottle caps, magazines, empty matchbooks, pennies, junk mail, coffee grinds, pencil stubs. She was trying to stop time from passing, to save the last moments of her childhood, because she knew it was over, that it had ended when she was looking somewhere else, and it was too soon. She would pull her chair by a window, look out on the garden, and clutch the armrests with her hands like a passenger convinced the plane is going down.

She wouldn't do her laundry, and her clothes gradually became dull and worn, like old coins. Finally Anne sent the girls out grocery shopping, and while they were gone she went into Olivia's room and gathered up the soiled garments, the shirts and jeans, the panties, the socks, and brought them down to the basement, where she stuffed them into the washer. When Olivia came home and found a pile of clean clothes on her freshly made bed, neatly folded and still warm from the dryer, she shook her head angrily, picked up the entire pile, and threw it on the filthy floor. After that she locked her door behind her whenever she left her room.

The doctor warned that if she became sick again it might hurt her. She became sick again; there was another sudden fever that attacked her, another day spent on her knees before the toilet in her bathroom, convulsed by dry heaves, and then a night of shaking in her bed.

She awoke the next day with cramps so terrible that she spent the morning lying on her back, wincing through her mother's gentle massage. By midmorning spots of blood had appeared. After lunch she felt a little bit better, and as three o'clock approached she decided she was well enough to wait in the living room for Marian to come home from school. Her water broke as she was walking gingerly down the stairs. It was several weeks early. Anne found her, legs drenched, sitting on the landing; she drove the girl to the hospital immediately, and Holiday met them there.

The baby was stillborn three hours later. Neither mother nor monster ever saw the child, an unnamed girl, a daughter; the small, flesh-soft corpse was removed before Olivia could shake off the first drops of the deep and dreamless sleep of her anesthesia.

4

When she awoke and her mother explained, she turned her white face to the wall. Marian sat with her, holding her hand and gently stroking her arm, until a nurse asked her to leave and gave Olivia another needle to sleep by. A week later she was allowed to come home.

For three days in mid-February she hid in her room and grieved, and Marian stayed home from school and waited with her. On the first day she delivered arguments for her agony, charges that took hairpin turns, backed up in cul-de-sacs of tears, stopped, stuttered, and then started at the beginning again. On the second day she projected herself into an imaginary future, in which everyone was always staring at her. On the third day she just shook, as if her body had been inhabited by primitive devils, and as evening fell Marian swore she saw her sister levitate slightly above her bed, rising above the mattress by the force of a negative ecstasy.

That night she locked herself in her room immediately after dinner and didn't come out again until the next morning. Marian couldn't say how it happened, but Olivia came to some kind of agreement with herself during the night. At breakfast her voice was still unsteady, but she had weight again, as if she had just decided to give it to herself. If anyone asked how she was she would say, Fine, I'm fine. That afternoon she cleaned her room and began to put her things in boxes, which she carefully labeled and then carried to the attic.

A week passed. The last day was grey, and bitter cold. A grey day, and as cold as could be. Sometime in the evening Olivia used the telephone, but no one knew whom she called; Marian picked up the phone by accident and heard her say, Yes, tonight . . . Yes, I'll be waiting, but she apologized and hung up again before she heard another voice. Just before midnight she knocked softly on the girl's door and said, Olivia? It's me.

It's all right, said Olivia. You can come in. She was sitting on the edge of her bed, fully dressed except for her shoes, which sat on the floor by her feet. Next to them was a small suitcase, packed until it bulged. Her canvas book bag, also full and buckled tightly shut, was on the bed beside her. What's this? said Marian.

I'm . . . going to leave. I'm leaving tonight. Olivia nodded sharply, and her best earrings swayed violently, until one became entangled in a lock of hair. She turned her head slightly to the side, reached up, and straightened it with unconscious fingers.

Where are you going?

I can't really tell you. I don't really know. Someone's coming to take me away.

Who is it?

I can't tell you that either. No one. She shook her head. I don't mean to make this too mysterious. It's just that I shouldn't say.

Marian walked over and sat beside her on the bed and briefly stroked her hair. When are you leaving?

About half an hour.

What do I tell Mom and Dad?

Tell them whatever. You can tell them the truth. Olivia lowered her lashes and stared at her feet, which had begun swinging slightly above the floor like the pendulum of a novelty clock. And if Wilson comes back, tell him I said I was sorry about the baby. I mean, I'm sorry it happened.

. . . .

Marian, said Olivia. I love you, too. You're the best sister. After I'm gone I want you to take care of this house. You know what I mean.

I know, I will, said Marian. She put her arms around the sadly smiling girl and held her. Olivia touched her sister's chin with the soft tips of her fingers. Neither sister seemed to find the night quite real; certainly Marian never really believed for a moment that Olivia was on the verge of some mystery ride, in a mystery car, to nowhere in particular. If she had she might have tried to stop her, or tried to join her, but it all seemed so peculiar, so quick: there was Olivia, there were her bags, and there, across the room, was a large grey-white moth attached by its forelegs to the window screen, its sail-shaped wings beating softly as it wistfully studied the light inside.

Well, I'd better go down, Olivia said. She stood up from the bed, slipped her shoes on, and picked up her bags. Marian checked to make sure the house was asleep and then waved her sister forward. They headed down the stairs without looking around.

It was an overcast night, and the porch lights were off. Olivia set her bags down and then sat on the front stoop; Marian sat beside her, her feet pulled up beneath her, so that while one girl sat with her hands in her lap, the other hugged her knees. It was cold. What did you bring? Marian asked.

Some clothes, mostly. A few pictures. You know . . .

Do you have any money at all?

Olivia paused, embarrassed, and then briefly shook her head. Wait here. Marian went into the house; a minute later she was back with her hand clasped tightly around a small roll of bills, which she slipped into her sister's jacket pocket. Thank you, said Olivia. Marian nodded.

A little later a pair of headlights appeared at the bottom of the drive and started slowly up towards them, winking as they passed behind a row of trees. Marian glanced back at the house to make sure her parents hadn't woken; all the windows were dark. Olivia stood up and sighed deeply. Here we go, she said, her voice toneless from tension. The next moment the car was at the door.

The lights shone in Marian's eyes, blinding her so that she couldn't see the driver; but she could tell that it was a long black Cadillac, as big and dark as the night itself, befinned and broad-shouldered, with sleek chrome styling and Texas plates. Olivia's bright eyes were fixed on the windshield, thrilled; the engine throbbed quietly. Then the passenger door opened. She looked at her sister, kissed her cheek, and started towards the car. When she reached it she stopped, turned, waved, and then climbed inside and shut the door. The car started forward, and as it passed Marian saw her sister's profile through the window, and, across the seat, the small, sparrow-silhouette of the driver. In a moment they were gone.

5

I'm sorry, Marian said when she was done. I'm really so sorry. She paused for a moment and looked down at the table in deference to the expression I wore. I know, she said. It isn't fair. But the thing is, in the end Olivia decided she just didn't want to get too good at suffering. I heard the boiler in the basement start up, and the sound of hot water making its way into the radiators.

Where is she now? I asked.

I don't know. That was about a month ago, and no one knows. No phone calls, no postcards, radio silence. It was like a ship sailing off into the fog and disappearing. So my parents called the police, they called everyone they could think of, our congressman, everything, and they call again about once a week. But . . . she's gone.

There's got to be something.

What? she said. Aside from that? I mean, the girl just left. I'm sorry. She sighed. Her face was flushed with sympathy. I had a thousand thoughts; they swirled like tea leaves in boiling water. Seventeen years, it was impossible. At the end of days there lies a dump, where pigeons land and pick at scraps. I would appeal, send a letter, illus-trated with hideous demons on every page, tear-stained and obscene with rage and regret. I would get going, as if to escape being pelted by the stones and clods of dirt that were being thrown by . . . who was it? Who was it? I saw the man.

You know I could help you, Marian said gently.

Help me? I said.

We could use each other, you know, she said, and I realized that there in the plain, bright kitchen she was petitioning me. Stay with me here, just for a little while. Let me tell you . . . . Olivia won't be coming back, but she left me with something to do. I was waiting for you, because she wanted us to help each other. Her voice became thin and strained as she spoke. Listen to me, she said. She was so frank that I wondered if it was possible that we were actually speaking, or if I weren't taking every one of her words wrong, as if in some prepos-terous lapse in language. I knew about you. I watched you talking to Olivia at our party. I knew. She told me the rest. She was my sister: she told me everything, she talked about you all the time—all the time. At first I thought it was part of her dreaming, or she was teasing me, but you know what? I thought I heard singing in the garden one night. That was a while before you two met. I wasn't sure—and then later when she said you made songs up all the time, I thought, maybe. She had so much to say that I started to believe her.

What did she say?

Marian bent her closed mouth up in a smile. Just listen for a second, will you? Also, I saw you one night, down by the gazebo, running around. She told me you once lived in it, and then you had to leave. I know why, too. You have no idea what he does. He told her she wasn't going to have that baby, and she didn't. She made an Oh! of utter frustration, dropped her fists onto the table and expelled a burst of pent breath through lips made pale by compression.

Olivia would—

Olivia had you, she said abruptly.

At that there was quiet in the kitchen. She was tired, her eyes fell, and she yawned. It seemed like the last breath of the night, like the only gallon of air left in the world, and I thought she would use it to swallow me whole, would actually consume me, so I braced myself. Instead she pushed herself back from the table, stood up, yawned again, and shook herself. Then she asked me to meet her the following night, in the garden, my own, my garden. I walked her to the foot of the stairs, where she turned, touched my cheek, and with an impossible smile said: You know I'm a monster.

6

She hadn't told me what time she would appear, or where I should wait, and I thought as I sat beneath the wet leaves of a big tree that she might have been kidding, or lying, or delaying, or dreaming, or plotting, or preparing to have me taken away. All that day I had been shaken by passing possibilia. They split my sentences like kindling, they splintered my thoughts. A wet smile, a bare leg, a loose bracelet. Those are verses that were her thighs.

It was a cold evening; there was a wind rushing through the yard on its way I don't know where; it had started at the head of the river a thousand miles north, picking up notes from its travels and dropping them into the trees in their backyard, where they made a rustling in the leaves as they landed. I think it was a country's worth of labor left exhausted at the end of the day. I pondered what she'd told me the night before. It made such sense I was convinced it was true. Finally, I saw movement at the back of the house, an open door and spindles of light around Marian's thin legs and skirt, and then the light was extinguished. A moment later I found her shadow in the garden, moving among the trees, disappearing, and emerging again on the grass; I could see her head and shoulders in delicate silhouette against the final, fading azure of the winter sky, and I thought at once of pointing it out to Olivia, who was not there.

With a last measured guess at her loyalties I watched her walk towards me, moving confidently through my fiefdom like royalty paying a visit from a larger land. She strolled right past, wearing a grey jacket and a black scarf around her throat. When she'd gotten a few yards farther into the chilly darkness I softly spoke her name. She didn't jump. I thought she would. She turned back towards me, unerring in her direction, took a few steps towards my voice, and then stopped. So I stood up out of the darkness, rose up, and motioned to her. No, she said in a hushed voice, farther away from the house. Without any hesitation, without even a hint of presumption, she took my hand in hers and led me back to a bench by the flower beds.

That night was the first of her thousand and one, and it began with her telling a story she called Too Small to Count. On successive nights we met after dinner out on the road by the end of their driveway, and she took me into town in her mother's car; we'd sit in a coffee shop, or perch on the bars of the jungle gym in the elementary school playground, and once she made me spend an evening strolling among the moonlit stones of a cemetery. Every night she recited another chapter; they went back to her earliest childhood, an enormous catalogue, replete with frame tales and embeddings, that she'd collected like a mirror Scherezade, not to save her life but to end his. There was A Glass of Whiskey, and The Telephone Call That Never Was, and The Bathing Suit That Revealed Too Much, itself part of the much longer History of the Lost Vacation; and then there was an unhappy cycle of stories about boyfriends, beginning with Johnny from Atlanta, through A Friend of a Friend, and ending with Mike Who Was Black. Olivia was a character in most of them, an implicit accomplice, a goad or a witness. I used to shiver whenever her name was mentioned, and Marian, who never denied or downplayed my sentiments, would generously pat my knee, or cast a phrase or two for me to reach. I sat by her and followed her winding entertainment, and thought constantly of our Dunyazade, and how she would have listened, were it possible.

Marian had a theory of everything, tangled explanations of her father and mother, her sister and herself, which she recast and renewed every day. She was perpetually, finally understanding things, and the clauses and lemmas multiplied out into the farthest reaches of her researches, always ending just where my instincts ended, the equation balanced by subtracting Holiday. I listened to her and admired her for her resolve, for her cleverness and her ability to play in and out of her father's law; in comparison I was a crude and unpolished thing.

She took me for a state of nature, a force she could be friendly with and harness: water, wind, Wilson. So she studied me. She would propose a situation—a stolen bicycle, a town fair, the vice principal of the junior high school—and then ask me into it, to see what would happen. Most often what happened was madness, but a madness she understood: we were very different, Marian and I, but we had lessons for each other, and we wanted to learn; what's more we had a common object that gave our learning a foothold in the world, and we were close. There was a cast of relations, a page of dramatis personae, each wearing a little description like the tail on a mouse: the King, his wife, a soldier, a messenger, a monster. Marian and I were up for the same part, and had decided instead to split it.

So I came to know two girls, where once I hadn't known any. As I learned the second, of course, the first seemed to change—not to become lesser—she would never be less than the only girl—but she took on more edges and angles, like a ruby that has been rotated so that the cuts on its underside show. One day when she was in the sixth grade, for example, Olivia was late returning from school. When at last she showed up, just before dinner, she announced that she had been saved on her way home.

Saved? her mother asked. What happened? Are you all right?

I'm good, said Olivia. And now that I've accepted the Lord Jesus Christ into my heart . . .

Anne questioned her carefully and then called Holiday. The next day a group of fundamentalist Methodists that had set up in a storefront in town received a visit from an attorney for the city, and while Olivia cried for a few days, and worried over the fate of her parents' souls for a few more, it wasn't long before she gave up praying and threw away the pamphlets that she'd carried home in the pages of her social studies textbook. She refused to talk about the episode ever again, nor would she take any teasing about it.

On another occasion, Marian told me, her little sister had joined some friends in a kissing contest in a clearing in the town woods. She was about thirteen at the time, and she chose as her partner another girl, a tomboy named Liz, a Liz like mine. They kissed like lovers; they lasted an hour, and they won.

7

One Sunday evening a week before Easter, Marian and I took a bench in a park overlooking the river. She seemed to be in a difficult mood—she scowled at me even before she sat down—and I asked her why. I don't feel great, she said. I feel soggy, and my tits hurt. Okay? But when she spoke of her mother her hands beat rapidly in her lap, and she began to rock back and forth in her seat. You see how perfect she is, how well bred. I could squat and piss in the living room at a dinner party and all she'd do is apologize. Well . . . my mother's all right. She's just a little scared. She'll be much better off when he's gone.

She stared out at the river, her body bent over her legs for warmth. The wake from a passing barge, long since converted into small waves, broke quietly against the bank. Where does she come from, your mother? I asked.

I don't know, said Marian. Ha. Really, I don't know, I have no idea. I think my father invented her, made her out of colored paper and paste. Then she was silent, as if she were reflecting on the craft that went into the fashioning of her mother.

At length I said, Maybe we should go, and started to stand.

Wait, wait, she said. I want—

She reached into her pants pocket and pulled out a penknife, fumbling with her cold fingers as she tried to open the small silver blade. At last she slid a thumbnail into the new moon-shaped groove at the thicker edge and managed to unfold it. Then she reached quickly for my hand, turned it face up, and took my index finger in her fist until a short, reddened inch protruded—and before I could say a word she'd stabbed down at it. I yelped in pain and pulled my hand

176

away, staring at the red line of blood that had immediately welled up on my fingertip. As I watched, it began to dribble down the side like crimson syrup.

—Marian made a short squeak: I looked up to find involuntary tears in her eyes. She sucked her wet breath in. Hold out your hand, she said. She put her bloody fingertip on mine and squeezed them together until I could feel her hot pulse throbbing; warm drops of mixed blood dripped down to the leg of my pants, where they made small black spots. She stared at our hands as if she hoped they would fuse. My finger grew numb. Finally she relaxed her grip and wiped her hand roughly on her jeans. Now we're brother and sister, she said. All right?

Then she reached into her jacket and drew out a pair of books, one slightly smaller than the other, both anonymous in the darkness. I have something to give you, she said. I wasn't going to, but I figured I should. Just so you understand. She put the books in my lap, then stood up and started to walk away, but before she'd gotten ten feet into the night she stopped, turned her shadowed face to me, and said:

Now I'm in you and you're in me
I'm in you and you're in me
I'm in you and you're in me.

8

I've mentioned Olivia's diary before. She began it when she was a little girl, almost as soon as she had learned to write, and as the years passed she had collected the books as she filled them, placing them in a box which she hid on top of her closet. A few weeks after we met she finished the last page of one, added it to the treasury, and began writing in the volume I'd left her among my first gifts. She wrote in it almost every evening, and for the half hour or so that she spent sitting up at the head of her bed scribbling down the day's thoughts I used to distract myself by reading one of her books (I remember a strange substitution of concept for substance that occurred one night when, while leafing through her dictionary, I came upon the word *gloaming* while the thing itself was waiting outside), or uselessly multiplying numbers on her calculator, or simply staring out the window until she would close the covers, put the book away in her desk, look up with a small, comely smile, and say, Okay. Over here.

In it was every story she wanted to save—I remember her pausing in mid-anecdote to dig up an early volume, which she used to check a fact or a feeling—and from time to time I would remember that on a shelf behind her closet door there lay an image of herself, as she saw herself, a shroud of my girlfriend's writing. I was, of course, hugely curious about what she had said, and if I stopped myself from sneaking a look while she was out of the room, it was as much because I was afraid she would come in and catch me as because I felt honor-bound not to steal her reflection. It was just the sort of thing that would have made Olivia furious with me—so much so that it hadn't even occurred to me to look for them when I went through her room. I wouldn't have found them anyway; as soon as Olivia had driven off Marian went back into the house and took them before her father could find them.

I sat in my room in the basement later that night, with the earlier book in my hands and my hands in my lap, and tried to decide whether or not to read it. First I turned it over and gazed at the unbroken binding, and then I set it down on my thigh. I even opened the cover and found her name and a beginning date on the frontispiece, and the sight of her handwriting made my breath wet, because I loved it, but I shut the book again before I could read on. It wasn't that I wanted to preserve her privacy; still, the thing stayed closed on my lap and lay there mute for a few minutes, because I was terrified. When I'd worked up my courage I opened it again.

APRIL 16. In school today someone told me I was too nice. Another spring—Shit. What are you going to do, Olivia?—Be stronger, be smarter, waste less time, be more patient, eat better, try not to let it get to you, have a good summer.—But you have no friends, really, you don't know anyone. Why not? It wasn't made for you. Mom says I'm just fine, but she doesn't know.

MAY 7. No one is going to do anything to me that I don't want, because I won't let them. No one is going to do anything to me at all, because I won't let them. Today some girls were dancing in the cafeteria during lunch, dancing to the radio—I watched from the back and I was thinking, I wish I could do that. Freak.

MAY 20. There's something weird happening in the garden.—I think there's someone out there. Last night I couldn't sleep, so I went out onto the patio in the dark. I heard a boy's voice singing a song back by the pool, the pond. I want to know who it is. Everything's grown big and wild—it's wonderful. It makes me want to—I don't know, I like it. Mom's happy, Marian laughed at me because I tried to ride my bicycle up to the front door, up the stairs.

JUNE 2. Sick in bed. So bored I could scream.

JUNE 12. He came into my room late last night while I was trying to get to sleep again, or trying to stay awake, I can't tell anymore. Whisper quiet, no birds. I looked up and he was sitting on the edge of my bed, kind of staring. I remember him from our party. He touched me, very gently, and I thought I would just about jump straight up and hit the ceiling. I felt crazy right away. He said he lived here, and then he left. I wasn't scared, I was so ready, and I thought, What is wrong with you? You're very fucked up.—But I'm feeling so fierce, I could just tear right into him, I want to sting him like a bee. It makes me laugh. —Come back, come back. I'll give you . . . presents

> pineapples
>
> parrots in silver cages.

JUNE 17.—Today there was a map of the world on my desk. I unfolded it on my bed and thought about where to go. Paris, of course, and Rome—but also Sri Lanka, to live in the tea fields, New Guinea and all over Africa.

JUNE 19. Well it happened last night at last. It hurt a little, not a lot. My own bed, late, late at night—he was there. I knew he would come—I was calling him all day, thinking about him hard. He gave a little speech, like he had to explain first. I just wanted to get on with it, so I kind of grabbed him. Shameless. A little fumbling at first, but then it was okay. I didn't realize it would go so far up.

My stomach was making noise all night. I hope he didn't notice.

JUNE 30. He does love to talk. Sometimes I find myself saying things without thinking, and then I stop and say to myself—Was that you? So I feel like I can do anything.

He tells me stories, pulls me along with this voice he gets. I can't believe some of the things he says. I worry sometimes that I'm just going to go under in the dark, and I'll never come back up—so I get mad, and he doesn't understand.

JULY 2. He does this kind of—thing sometimes, it's like, suckling. Funny word. It's so nice I can't stand it. When he's inside it's like a circuit that's always open is suddenly closed, the power can jump across that gap; then the bulb starts to glow, the little clapper on the bell starts to quiver, getting ready to ring. I lean back and think, wherever you're going I'm going too—and then we go.

I like the way he smells.

JULY 10. When Daddy came home tonight he called me into his office, very serious about something—but then I thought about W.—we'd just finished doing it, in the middle of the day when the house was empty, really hard, so I was still aching from it—and I smiled, and when he looked at me I started laughing, I couldn't help it. He was mad. I wish I had a bigger bed.

JULY 18. Six days late. I feel heavier already, can feel it churning up and collecting like gelatin.—It's scary. I knew right away, knew the night it happened, and I knew I was going to keep it, too.—It's ours, and if I don't tell anyone they can't take it away. Sooner or later W. can come out, maybe move in here for real. Hiding him is such a strain—but everything's going to change, it's all going to be better. Daddy won't like it, but he won't be able to do anything.—It's a revolution in the petting zoo.

JULY 30. I think W. knows, but he hasn't said anything. I don't know what he thinks. He's paying a lot of attention to me, even though I got mad at him this morning.—He got mad back but an hour later he was apologizing—but I didn't want to talk, I just wanted him to hold me for a while. I don't know what he's thinking, almost ever. —I don't know what to do.

AUGUST 4. Sunny day, sat on the back patio. W. very sweet today, snuck up and brought me flowers from the garden, with this look on his face that made me want to cry, or yell. He has no parents anymore, so he needs me. Don't blow it, you can do it.
—I feel like a jukebox, flashing lights and happy music.

AUGUST 17. Olivia Miller. Olivia Miller. Olivia Miller. Olivia Miller.

AUGUST 20. It was worse than I thought. How can Daddy yell at me now? I know what he's thinking, that I'm stupid, that I'll ruin my life. But W. showed me ghosts dancing in the backyard, and said everything was all right. I did see them, too.

SEPTEMBER 15. No control.—Dreaming and dreaming, and floating—I can't feel myself anymore.

OCTOBER 2. Marian knows who it is, of course, and she says I have to send him away or else I'm just going to fall apart. Just tell him he has to go, he can come back later. If he loves me—no, she said, because he loves you. She said she'd take care of me. She said she'd tell him if I wanted but I said I'd better—I need just a few days more.

OCTOBER 6. He left, I didn't give him any choice, I was scared. He hates me—Everyone does.

OCTOBER 20. So W. is gone, and now I don't know if he was ever here. I asked Marian and she said, Yes, of course. Did I think I was Mary? She gave me a long hug, said everything will be fine—I don't know that. I have to start classes at this school—Marian calls it Miss Andrews' School for Wayward Girls, and makes me laugh—but I'm falling behind and I have to go.

NOVEMBER 12. Another fit today, like I was six feet away from the world. No one saw. W. gone, Marian helps, as much as she can. There was a man standing at the bus stop today who looked at me, fat as I am, and said something so disgusting I can't even write it down. Argh. I wanted to go up to him and just pull my clothes off so he could see.

JANUARY 1. New Year. Watched it on TV with Marian, soon to be an aunt, she was sweet enough to stay home.

JANUARY 12. Daddy came into my room again this evening, so angry I thought he was going to hit me—he just stormed in without knocking, when Mom and Marian were out of the house. You cannot have that baby, he said—You will not—We'll send you away. Do you know what they do to girls with babies?—No school, no job, home forever. He said, when you were little we could take care of you, but you're a big girl now, and we're not going to help you with this, if you insist on going through with it. I said, It's too late anyway, I'm seven months in, and he just looked at me and said, This is my house, and you are my daughter. You will not have that baby.

JANUARY 17. I think my food is being poisoned, and I think I know who it is. The baby is kicking almost all the time. It wants to put its foot through my stomach and break out, like a cartoon chick out of a cartoon egg. No one ever wonders how the egg feels about it. I'm tired all the time but I can't sleep.

JANUARY 19. [There was nothing written here, but she had scrawled a crude picture of a big dog.]

JANUARY 20. There are dead animals in the yard. It's from Daddy—I think he's crazy—I think he hates me. The flesh comes off the bones, and the bones come off the marrow. I keep finding blood in my dreams. He's going to kill me.

FEBRUARY 4. I feel so sick.

It ended there, on that hard syllable; and I knew at once why bombers blow up banks, why tornadoes touch down in trailer parks, why the windows on a burning room weep.

9

There were eight empty glasses on the table. The jukebox was quiet for the first time in an hour. Marian's head was lowered over the table, her chin resting on her fists while she looked out blankly at a dime that was resting in a thin slick of fluid next to an ashtray. I can't stand it. I can't stand it, she said. It's so fucked up.

10

I took her down to the gazebo. We sat on the stairs, facing the house, and I drew an imaginary line with my forefinger, as if I were laying out the lines of a playing field. The house is his, but the garden is still mine, I said. From the edge of the patio to the bottom of the yard is a free zone. That's fair, isn't it?

Of course, she replied.

Marian, I want it proved, I said, and rose to my feet. So we're going to try him here tonight. Okay? She put her gloved hands on her knees and then stood up by pushing down until she rose, like a toy girl with mechanical joints, and we walked hand in hand out onto the lawn. A few yards away there was a small hillock; I remembered having to strain to push a mower up it the spring before, and then suddenly leaning back to stop it from getting away from me as it rolled down the short slope at the other side. We made our way to the top, turned, and faced the grounds. Marian held her hands clasped before her. Can I begin? she asked, and I gestured in deference. Ladies and gentlemen of the jury, she said suddenly, addressing a row of hydrangea bushes that I had planted the previous summer—Wait. She stopped and took a breath to keep her voice from shaking. Ladies and gentlemen of the jury. Your honor, she said, and looked respectfully towards a rhododendron. My associate and I—she gestured towards me—are here today to put a case against one Holiday Miller, who is my father, and his . . . father-in-law. She stood with her back straight and spoke sternly and precisely.

Mr. Miller is accused of being a bad man, she continued, emphasis on the penultimate word, which she dragged out until it bleated. I suppressed a snort of laughter, and she smiled quickly. There's so much evidence against him that I don't know where to begin . . .. She looked at me encouragingly, but I remained silent. Something fluttered in a tree top a few yards away. All right, she said. This is serious. To begin with, he drove my sister away.

A girl I loved, I said. The rhododendron nodded in a breeze.

Marian interrupted her advocate's pose and turned to me. Yes. She loved you too. And I always approved of you. She'd never had a boyfriend before, and I was so proud of her for having done that, all on her own. In a few years she'd have been just another one of his . . . nothing. The judge and jury had become bushes again; Marian's voice grew hard in premature defense of a complaint. I'm sorry you had to leave. She was so scared of him she didn't even know. Well. She turned back to address the jury again, unconsciously smoothing her skirt with her hands. Then he made her lose her baby.

184

My daughter, I said. The last syllable turned into a blue moth, flew upwards out of my mouth, and got away.

That would be enough, Marian said. It would be more than enough, but we're not done. Look at my mother—she was suddenly louder, her voice rising until it was almost shrill and I was afraid that someone would hear her. How could she have married him? She asked me as if she wanted to know and thought I could tell her. If she hadn't I would not have ever been born. I don't care. Look at me. I did, and I was surprised to find a girl my age standing there, thin and temperamental, her features narrowed by anger. Go on, she said sharply to me.

He burned me out of my garden, I said. But that's nothing, because Olivia . . .

That's right, said Marian firmly.

There was a nimbus around the moon, a magnified mist of white with a faint, ice-blue ring in it. I hadn't noticed it earlier. My colleague had paused to consult her notes. After a moment she spoke again: What is a bad man? she asked. A bully is a bad man. A boy might tilt up the world until it faced over him. A daughter might take a sword against him and prove her position. Say it, just say it.

While we waited we went back to the bench, and Marian picked up my hand and held it tightly. Open and shut, she said gaily. It won't be long. After a minute had passed I got up again, walked briskly over to the hydrangeas, and addressed the leftmost bush directly.

Have you reached a verdict? I paused. And what is your verdict? I reached down, plucked a single early bud from a branch, and brought it over to her. Out blew my nervous, enormous breath. All right. I peeled back the bright green carapace, and the petals below were small and tightly packed. Then I began to draw them off one by one, letting them drop to the ground at our feet until I reached a point where they were so tiny that I had nothing left to grasp. I split the remaining budlet with my thumbnail and glanced at the result: by the moonlight I could see a creeping black spot, a sort of signifying stain, in the deepest heart of the flower. I showed it to Marian. Guilty, she said matter-of-factly.

Guilty, I said.

Okay— as if she'd just confirmed a law of nature. What's the sentence? She went over to the rhododendron. Her hands were clasped at her waist. She leaned over the bush and listened. After a few seconds had passed, she suddenly rose again and clapped her hands. Yes, she said excitedly. That's what we were hoping. She straightened up and turned back to me. Well, she said:

I can't say it but I know what it is
I can't say it but I know what it is
I know, I know, I know what it is.

11

The verdict, you see, was mine, and it was a mere thing, but the sentence and all its meaning was hers. A boy can spend a year in school, in and out of class again, and no one will teach him: Violence has a way of its own, with rules of proportion, plot and design. That is violence. Vengeance is a perfect circle, as axiomatic and bold as any figure found in Euclid's abstract space. And that is vengeance. We make justice ourselves, like we make a house, with an eye to the distribution of our practical actions and the clearest view, and then we take our place in it and live. And that is justice. I hated Holiday and gave him every fault. He had thieved the one thing I had ever earned, and I would right the world by ruining him. My side was therefore chosen. But my jealousy and rage were incapable of anything; so the actions that followed were lessons Marian taught me in the arts of human agency, an education for which, in the end, I will always be grateful.

12

One paper-thin afternoon Anne went through Holiday's dresser drawers in search of a cotton shirt of her own that she thought she might have misfiled on laundry day. On the bottom of the bottom drawer, beneath a maroon sweater that he never wore, she found a magazine, a glossy, glaring thing that I'd already seen three times before. She wore a look of utter disgust as she carried it away, and for several days she came and went in the house without saying much to anyone, wearing an expression as if there were a very faint sound in her ears, a ringing that bothered her.

She knocked on Marian's door one night later that week and asked her if she wanted to go for a drive, and when Marian said Sure, she went downstairs and waited silently in the foyer for the girl to get dressed and find her jacket. Where are we going? Marian asked when she came down a few minutes later, stopping on the bottom stair to pat her pockets for her gloves. All her mother said was, You don't need gloves. Let's go.

According to the girl they never stopped, they just drove and drove, south on the highway for forty miles or so, then around home again on a county road. And her mother spoke only once, and then just as they'd gotten to the farthermost point of their trip and were turning back; she'd pulled off the highway onto a frontage road, and the car was stopped for the first time, caught at a red light that hung over the blacktop like the glowing eye of an irradiated insect. Some distance out into the darkness a shimmering green and white sign showed the road ahead splitting in two.

Boo, said Anne.

When Marian turned to look at her she found someone she did not recognize. The light turned green, and the car started forward again.

13

The next day, as Holiday sat in his study, Anne knocked on his door. She held something rolled up in her hand, and held her hand at her hip. Yes? he said, and she crossed in. Holiday? He didn't look up, but his hand stopped writing.

Turn around, she said carefully. He swiveled his chair around with his feet; his hands grasped the armrests. He was in his shirt-sleeves, and his tie was undone, though it was still around his neck. All right. What is it? he asked impatiently.

What is this? She held the magazine up, but it was facing her, and he couldn't place it from the photograph on the back cover. He said, I— and then went silent and averted his eyes as he recognized it. I found this in one of your drawers, and I want to know why you have it, she said. She was on the verge of angry tears, and her voice quavered slightly, as if she was afraid.

I don't know.

You don't know?

I found it, he said.

You found it?

It was in Olivia's room. I found it after she left.

It was an answer so improbable and so apparently cowardly that at first she was at a loss for words. Oh, come on now, she said finally, with a disgust that he knew at once he couldn't answer. He stared at her through his glasses, reaching for an effect of clear, unblinking innocence that was somehow ruined by the bifocal line in his lenses. She turned around and left.

Out of the house, in a diner downtown, Marian and I ate ice cream and she remembered the magazine. Just as hard as a turtle's back, she said. It could have been all right, except that girl, with all that paint . . .

I described the look on her mother's face, her eyes held carefully on him, her skin insufficient to say, and asked her if it wasn't too much. She grimaced and shook her head. I . . . poor Mommy, I know. But she sat by and watched as all this happened. I don't blame her, but I do.

Will she be all right?

Best for all concerned, she replied brightly. Trust me: I know it looks bad, but think of what a mess my house is. Something has to change, or else my father will just take over again. See? And he will, you know. She bent over and spooned the last of the chocolate syrup into her mouth, then licked a blot of goo from her lips as she shook her head.

188

He can't be trusted with anything. They say—they, people in town—that my father had a partner once, years ago when Olivia and I were little. They set up a practice together, and then my father decided he didn't want him around, so he cheated him out of everything, cheated him bad, and he had to leave town. I don't know, all I remember is this strange little man who used to come by the house, bringing presents. He had these tiny little hands and feet. His name was . . . something real plain, like Johnson, but that's not it. Something like that.

I asked her what she'd been looking for in Holiday's office that night, by then it seemed a year or more back, when another Marian, one I did not know, had let herself in after her parents had gone to bed and searched the place.

Magic books, she said, her eyes widening for effect. Spells and incantations, recipes, voodoo dolls, potions. My father is . . .

Just then a friend stopped by the table, a girl with chopped blond hair and dark circles under her eyes. She placed her hand on the tabletop and said a weary Hey, Marian. How are you?

Just all right, said Marian as she looked up.

The girl looked at me curiously but we weren't introduced; she waited for a moment while Marian eyed her expectantly, but she didn't have any more to say and in a moment she had made her good-bye and was gone. Under the guise of pretending to study the chalkboard menu above the counter Marian shot the briefest of disparaging glances at her retreating back, and then turned back to the table. She was a friend of Olivia's, she said. She's been spreading rumors all month, and she thinks I don't know. Maybe we should kill her too.

I was wondering how we might when Marian said, Jesus Christ, I was just kidding. Wilson? But by then I was watching the too bright sunlight out the window, watching the houses, the stores and churches dissolve in the midday like a fresh oil painting to which someone has taken a sponge soaked in turpentine, making a parti-colored smear on the far side of the glass, which, in my angry imagination, grew less and less substantial, until, at last, there was nothing left at all.

14

. . . on a bench by the brackish fish pond. She wore a pair of silver earrings and a bit of makeup. It was so cold that her breath steamed from her mouth, and she repeatedly lifted the side of an index finger to the tip of her nose to staunch an imaginary flow, a girlish gesture that made me think of the petals of invisible daisies. She was nervous and excited but she wouldn't say why, in any case not just yet. Instead she wriggled on her seat and said, Ask me something, go on.

Ask you what?

That's the point, I don't know.

I thought for a moment while she shivered impatiently, then sidestepped my lusterless imagination and gave her Olivia's question. What do you want to be?

An assassin, she said without hesitation, adding a short, violent nod for emphasis. I'm sorry, she went on, I just can't resist. Look what I got today. She dug deep into her coat pocket for something big and heavy—too big, in fact, to come out easily; it snagged on the lining, and for a few seconds she tugged and twisted, growing slightly frustrated, for her star actor had tripped over his entrance. At last a metal handle emerged in the grip of her small fingers, and then, with a final twist and pull, the long barrel of an enormous pistol appeared. She displayed it in her open hand, and I reached for it with one of those mechanical acts of taking that eight-year-old boys use to appropriate their friends' new toys. She gave it up, but her eyes remained fixed on the fat part of the casing as I held it heavily in my hand, raised it towards the house for a second, and then turned it towards the darkest part of the garden. Stick 'em up, I said softly. Across the lawn a boxwood reached for the sky. Bang. You're dead.

She smiled. Isn't it beautiful? I bought it from someone at school, she said. It was a lot.

It's big.

Yeah, I know. She seemed pleased with it. From her left pocket she withdrew a chocolate bar, already half-unwrapped. She broke off a chunk the size of her thumb and offered it to me. When I shook my head she shrugged and popped it quickly into her mouth. Shouldn't we use his? I asked.

We will, she said with some amusement, and took the pistol back. You will. It's a little too . . . symbolic? for me. I'll use this one.

15

Late that night, as I was lying restlessly on my pile of blankets in the basement, Olivia suddenly showed up in my mind, laughing at something I hadn't seen, holding her hands in fists at her waist. A little later in my sleep I was standing by a dresser in my room in Lincoln, and she came up to me, strong, naked, her skin vanilla, her lips and nipples pinkish red, flooding my dream-filled mouth with some sweet slippery substance. She had come to tell me she was leaving, and I begged her for one last hug, but her face fell, she frowned, and refused me sadly; someone was waiting for her. I watched her through the mirror above the dresser as she slipped out the door. When I woke the next morning I found a familiar throbbing halfway down the sheets, and a small breath-belaboring pebble in my throat.

16

There was a nut-brown bird singing in the bare branches of a tree, amid the stems of grey stalks and twigs that multiplied into the grey sky, splitting again and again like nerves stripped of their flesh, with no message to bring, no motion left upon which to insist. The bird sang, its chree-chree, its reet-reet, while Anne stood by a cold window and listened to the unbearable noise. The world was unreal and had always been so, and as the bird sang its last note and suddenly flew out of the branches in a flurrying, downward arc that sent it out of sight, she underwent a fit of fatidic panic; the house upended before her eyes, flipping over like the image in a *camera obscura*, while she hung down helplessly. She froze until, a few moments later, it had passed, and then backed away, leaving a patch of fog from her breath and prints from her sweating fingertips on the glass, where they lingered for a second or two before melting away.

17

You hate her sometimes. You don't know what happened, what to doYou want to yell at her, you want to kill her, you want to bring her back. It's okay . . . It's just you're angry. You want to touch her again, she could be doing anything, now. It's okay. I know all about it, it doesn't mean anything. You should have seen her when you left. It's okay.

18

Something unexpected was next. One night before bed Anne came down the stairs in her bathrobe and found Holiday in the living room, sitting with a book. She gently said his name and retied her robe. He didn't respond at all: he simply turned the page. She asked him to speak to her. He had his head cocked slightly back and turned to one side, while he stared down his nose at the page. He pushed his glasses up, he clamped his pipe in his teeth. She waited for a few moments and then asked again. His large head rose from the paper, his eyes fixed upon her, and he refused, the simple words—No, I will not—inducing a fit of unexpected temper that brought him out of his seat. She ran from the room; he sat down again. She was back through the door a moment later, and she supplicated him again, unaware that her robe had come half undone, revealing the sky-blue silk of her nightgown. She called him by a pet name as if the intimacy of invoking it would soften him. Instead he looked her up and down, made a harrumph, and pretended to go back to his reading, though of course the trembling page was filled with meaningless black ink spots.

She spent that night in the guest room. When morning came she went into her daughter's room and spoke to her for a few minutes while Holiday hid behind the door to his bedroom and I hid in the attic. Soon after, Marian came upstairs to find me. When I walked out from behind a cardboard box—the label said: Olivia/elementary school—she was standing by a shadeless floor lamp, with a look on her face as if she'd just seen a deer get hit by a truck. My mother is leaving, she said at once. It's really happening. She said she should have done it a long time ago, she said she was sorry. With a thin hand she tucked her hair behind her ear, and she smiled weakly. I'm supposed to stay until school is done. So you and I . . .. She opened her arms for me. I went to her and she hugged me, rocking me gently, gently against her body for a few moments before she turned away and started for the door. Motes of golden dust that she'd kicked up when she'd come in streamed diagonally down in the currents of the attic air, infinitely fine grains endlessly pouring down into a pool before an unused wardrobe, like some magical wind-borne gift. I was still watching them when she walked out.

Anne's last scene with Holiday took place in the unlit wings, amid flats and pulleys, and a suitcase full of brightly colored costumes. It began with memories and accusations, short lines played fast, occasionally lapsing into unexpected rhyme—life with wife, for example, and daughter with water. When she finished there was music for a minute or two, cheap strings and a piano. Then there was a noise like a man falling off a ladder—the set shook slightly and the music stopped. The place was silent for a moment, and then the queen's voice started up; it floated out over the empty seats; she was delivering an unscripted soliloquy on the end of majesty.

An hour or so later she left; Marian helped her take her bags out, and I caught a glimpse of the two of them standing by the car. The girl was looking at her mother, and her mother was staring at the house, as if it were a tree that had strangled her hanging years. Holiday was in his study trying not to listen, and he didn't come out again until she was gone. Then he stood in the foyer and peered through the window beside the front door at the empty driveway, the bare sloping lawn, the line of trees shielding the house from the road in front, the blue, blue sky. When he turned back his face was pale and his hands shook at his sides.

Marian found me again soon after her mother left, and whispered hotly in my ear:

Mom's in the car and the car's on the highway
Mom's in the car and the car's on the highway
Once it went his way, now it goes my way
Mom's in the car and the car's on the highway.

19

She had left the three of us, he to his empty days, and Marian and me to him. Meticulous Holiday immediately began to set the house in order, as if he were preparing for some special event. He would stand in a room, looking over its arrangement carefully, and then fix it by moving a chair over to a precise place by a window, or clearing a coffee table of everything but an empty china bowl. He gave the impression that each adjustment was part of some elaborate recipe, and as it gradually became clear to him that Anne was not coming back he increased his efforts, and they became increasingly eccentric. Once I watched from the living room window as he went out into the garden and took a slow walk through the ravaged paths, the dry patches of burned grass, the fish pond, now covered with floating islands of bright green moss, the hard dirt where the herb garden had been, the scorch marks beside the gazebo where he had, in casting the stuff of my pared-down life into the flames, begun his end. He was collecting things here and there; from time to time he would stop, bend down, and examine a stone or a twig, and then, if it passed, place it carefully in his jacket pocket. Slowly and methodically he moved through the grounds, and when he was done he came back to the house and filled a glass jar with the fragments he had recovered, and then put the jar in the center of the kitchen table. He spent the next day cooking something foul-smelling, which he left in a pot in the refrigerator, and the day after that he went around the house and washed each window with warm water and vinegar, until the glass shined brightly, like silvery panes embedded in the walls.

As Holiday pursued his unlikely administration, Marian camped in the house like a loner beneath a highway overpass, gathering the few possessions she cared about around her and sleeping lightly. She did not allow her friends to call. Olivia's birthday was coming up, and we were waiting, restlessly, with little to do until then.

One night later that week I found myself distracted by a sudden clutching at my thoughts as I passed her room one night and help-lessly remembered the motion she used to make as she locked her door, how the fingers of one hand lay softly on the knob while with the other she slowly turned the bolt, as if to prolong the delicious sensation of enclosing herself with me inside. I stopped, and in my faint reverie I failed to hear Holiday starting up the stairs, and only awoke when the flicker of his shadow on the wall caught my eye. I had to throw myself into the linen closet and shut the door swiftly before me. I was sure he'd hear the noise, but he didn't; I could see him through the slats, making his way up the last few steps, his feet bare, his walk swaying, his face pressed down into his open hands. I couldn't hear anything but the sound of my own breath, I was so intent on controlling my gasps, but I watched him as he turned and stared at his daughter's door, facing half-away. His chest was heaving and his shoulders were shaking, and as I looked he pulled his hands from his face, slowly, the way a child will pull a bandage from a skinned knee; it was as if he were afraid he would strip the skin from his features, and I saw the shiny glint of tears melting on his wax-pale cheeks.

I said nothing to Marian about it. She and I intended to see to it that he knew, but only at last. The force that countered him and drew down such ill fortune had been hidden from him, a door shutting at the far side of a room he'd just entered, a telephone that stopped ringing as soon as he'd reached it; when the moment came, we would lift the walls and reveal ourselves, as children, as wild legislators.

20

Olivia's birthday fell on a Wednesday. She would have been, would be, seventeen. Marian and I planned a little celebration, and that evening we met whispering in the basement, set up an unsteady card table, lit a dozen and a half candles on a small store-bought cake, and wished her many many happy returns. Marian took her forefinger and dragged it through the white icing, and then, with a look of exquisite suffering, sucked the dollop off. With dim light below her face, eyes thick with thoughts.

All I ever wanted, she said. All I ever wanted was to have possession over   All I ever wanted was to be, you know   A charmed life   Love, she said. Family   My little sister and me, we were going to start a kind of tribe, just girls and boys. A nation of   It was in the woods, and we were going to   Make love, adventure. Little girls.

And that was me? I asked.

That was part of it, she replied.

21

Holiday went quietly to his room at around ten that night. Marian was sitting beside me at the top of the attic stairs, and when his door shut behind him she put her hands on my upper arm and squeezed. Soon afterwards the light beneath his door disappeared; she hit me gently on the side of my knee. We waited a long while, and then we rose up, tiptoed down the stairs, and entered Olivia's room. Well . . . Marian said. Here we go.

Her hands shook as she opened the door to the closet; she smiled quickly as she closed it upon herself. I heard a faint thud as she tripped over a box on the floor and fell backwards against the

196

wall. Okay! she whispered through the door. Go on! The room was pitch black. I held my breath, stood prepared for my accusation. My lungs were tight from frost. I climbed onto Olivia's bed, bed that we had broken in, and I began to bounce.

I had never shouted in that house. Hey! I shouted, and called him with a song that I sang out in long, slow measures:

If I were a monster, and you were a man
If I were a monster, and you were a man
Would you let me take your daughter
To the Sugartown dance?
Yo-dee-o-lay-ee-hoo!

I've got a good reason, and my sister's got a plan
I've got a good reason, and my sister's got a plan
We didn't ask for ransom
We're going to kill a man
Yo-dee-o-lay-ee-hoo!

I could hear Marian punctuating my words with muffled exclamations from out of the closet, a door-dampened Yeah!, a distant That's right! I was bouncing in a circle and I'd just come around to face the door again when I noticed Holiday standing a step or two into the room, holding a match up before his face and squinting around it. I was so possessed by my bouncing and yodeling that I hadn't heard him come in. The flame cast a small volume of ancient light around the room, a flickering field, not so much colored as drawing out the colors and forms of the furniture, the base of the wall, and a floor made round by shadows. He was barefoot, dressed in the bottom half of a pair of pajamas, and above his pale, puffy chest his features were smudgy and his dull eyes stared. He was as calm as could be, and he watched me with palpable exhaustion, standing so close that I heard his heart slowly throbbing. The convex form of the room was reflected in his wet eyes, and I could see myself represented there, my last face, a tiny light. He was entirely alone.

The flame burned down the matchstick and bit his fingertips, and he quickly shook it out and let it drop extinguished to the floor. The room was dark again. I could sense Holiday standing away from me, waiting for me to cease to be; I could hear his even breathing, and I knew at once, I immediately knew, that my monster's amorous trials were ending as finally as the last few frames of film flapping through a film projector.

Hm. He cleared his throat and hitched up his pants. At last he spoke. Of course. You came by my office You were wearing my tie. So it was you all along?

Yes.

Who are you? Fat Holiday, pursy Holiday, in his daughter's room with his daughter's murder-minded boyfriend. I stared. Answer me. He turned on her desk lamp, and then stepped outside of its dim, diluted light. Where is Marian?

I'm right here, she said. She stood in the dark doorway of Olivia's closet with the big gun weighing down her soft small hand. He gazed at her, but he didn't seem to see what she carried. Or perhaps he was very brave, or very stupid, or very—

You hate me, he said, as if he was merely mentioning it.

You don't know, she answered.

Olivia— but before he could finish I'd winced my ears shut: Marian had shot a hole through the window. Not much of the glass had broken. The air was stiff with the sweet smell of gunpowder. Holiday was suddenly sitting on the edge of the bed. I'm sorry, he said. I was wrong.

Marian stamped her foot and said, No.

He put his hands loosely on his knees, giving his shoulders a meaningless shrug. My daughters hate me. He looked up at me. Maybe you'll forgive me

Don't do that, said Marian. She was trying not to shake and she shook like a drunk; the barrel of her gun wobbled. My own wretched pistol had somehow found its way halfway into my front pocket, where it pressed against my hip. My hand was still on it, my forefinger resting against the trigger the way it would across my lips if I were trying to quiet him.

Instead he took a deep, storytelling breath. I tell you, he said, I made this place, and I wanted to keep it forever, like the pictures on Achilles' shield   to keep the houses, the towns, the scenes in the square, the weather in the sky   I would have liked to have died in a corner of my garden   wrapped in a blanket and nodding in the sunlight. Well, I'm an old man, with thankless daughters and a joyless wife. I demanded a little love from them   and they couldn't give it, because I demanded it. So I decided to unmake them   He shook his head sadly on his chest. I'm sorry, he said again. Pause, while outside Olivia wandered. Pause

What am I supposed to do with that? you said.

I don't know. Defeated candidate, losing pitcher.

Your face contracted and you twisted on your hip, drew back the hand that held the gun and feinted with it. Then you swore a nameless syllable and threw it at him as hard as you could, with your head down and your eyes squeezed tightly shut. He jerked to cover himself and the piece glanced off his forearm, skittered across the floor towards a corner of the room, and abruptly disappeared.

You were leaning against the wall where a chest of drawers had been, softly crying. He rubbed the sore spot on his arm and looked up at me, as if he were seeing me for the first time. Well. Here he paused for a moment, and then spoke again. Are you going to murder me?

I said, No.

Will you be forgotten?

Yes, I said.

He stood up, and Olivia's bed evaporated, like perfume Why? he asked, as if it were a gentle sort of examination.

I have nothing left, I answered. There was a crowding within me, a slow drip of shame in my heart of hearts.

Give it here. He held out his hand for my gun, and I gave to him like a payment. I know you, he said. Olivia's curtains turned to mist and vanished. I know all about you and what you've done. It's been enough. So you would bind your abilities up in a chest and sink it in the sea   He gestured with his hands to illustrate   House, stick, trunk, strap, water   You wanted to live with others as others live; but you can't, and you can't live alone I know you can't   I tried myself long before you came. Boy, let go, he commanded, his voice echoing in the room, because the room was suddenly empty. It's too late, let go anyway.

Where will I go?

Anywhere, nowhere   Just get away from here.

And then as if by some strange, uncommon force I felt my feet lift from the ground, and slowly I began to move across the floor-boards, passing through the door, floating down the shallow, softening staircase, its flower-patterned wallpaper walls streaming up and out of sight as I held onto a banister like the railing on the deck of a descending ship. I could hear Holiday roaring above me, as a room went by from below, and then a string of rooms; they were tilted and open like boxes, like balloons, reversing and replacing them-selves, giving up long forgotten fragments of careful speeches, stuck gestures, crayon drawings and clothes. In one I saw a woman with your mother's features sitting in a chair, nursing an infant, the right side of her shirt raised to expose her breast and the baby's mouth closed around its nipple. In a second a crystal decanter full of dark reddish liquor was floating a few feet above the carpet, bobbing and turning gently. Jones was standing in the middle of the next, neatly dressed and smiling broadly as he held a red-barreled fountain pen out in his hand. There were stray pages of music books, and telephone messages, and a souvenir fan from the state fair. With the sound of twenty years they all rushed past me, pulling at my clothes like wind. Holiday, bellowing and thrashing, had opened his bag and let them loose at last, and in a minute they were gone.

When I next noticed my place I found my shoes were wet through from the dew on the front lawn. You were standing beside me, your face flushed; you were still sobbing, gulping, shedding tears as you stared at the desolate house. I turned and followed your gaze, to the front steps and closed door, the balustrades, the sheltering trees towering above the eaves, the railings and the roof pitched into the sky, and the window to Olivia's room, dimly lit but forever empty of the girl we knew.

You had been holding my breath, and by the time I turned

around again you'd backed away and were gone with it, a small figure in blue jeans and a black sweater, running down the yard towards the bottom of the driveway, too quickly to say good-bye.

Marian, I have no way of knowing where you are, with whom or in what mood, but you're the only one who might still care to have this told. Your father lives in an empty house, with his empty head full of sleep and forgetfulness, and your mother is steadfastly against the past. And Olivia . . .

When I lit out I went looking for her, and I looked for a long, long time. I stopped in every town I passed through, I peered into every car, I poked down every alley, and I talked until my tongue swelled up and choked my throat. I suspect at last that she does not exist. Or perhaps she does and simply wants to be left alone. In any case she does not exist, except as a product of our mutual recollection—just as the position of a point on the far bank of a river can be fixed as the junction of two observers' gazes on the opposite side. The river is not time, or love, or sympathy; it's just a river, maybe the Mississippi. I can't tell.

So we're the last ones left, and this book is between us. Last night I put the final fat period in place, put my pen aside, and stacked the pages neatly on the side of my desk. Today I will send the whole thing away, and we will see. I hope you'll come upon it one pale, pale blue afternoon when you're idly browsing in a local bookstore.

Sister, the world I wished for has become extinct, and despite these notes what we now remember will soon be lost forever in impermanence; no one will ever know that once, a long time ago and nowhere, there lived a boy (not any boy, but me) and a beautiful young girl (not any girl, but my Olivia), whom he loved, utterly and endlessly. Now every park is public, and every girl has taken her kisses and run away, and no one knows what another one wants. So what was the time? What was it like? This is my last and best testimony: there was a warm glance, a bed with the covers drawn, a bit of lingering weight, an allowance made.

Now tell me, where do young boys and girls get the sweet and terrible bravery that moves them?